YULETIDE
COLD CASE
COVER-UP

JESSICA R. PATCH

LOVE INSPIRED SUSPENSE
INSPIRATIONAL ROMANCE

LOVE INSPIRED® SUSPENSE
INSPIRATIONAL ROMANCE

ISBN-13: 978-1-335-55463-5

Yuletide Cold Case Cover-Up

PLEASE RECYCLE
THIS PRODUCT IS RECYCLABLE

Recycling programs
for this product may
not exist in your area.

Love Inspired
22 Adelaide St. West, 40th Floor
Toronto, Ontario M5H 4E3, Canada
www.Harlequin.com

Printed in U.S.A.

There is therefore now no condemnation
to them which are in Christ Jesus.
—*Romans* 8:1

For those who do not feel worth forgiving...you are.

A special thanks to my agent, Rachel Kent;
my editor, Shana Asaro; my friend and author Susan L. Tuttle;
and my family. I appreciate you all so much
and couldn't do this without you. Thank you.

ONE

The Christmas season would never be the same—not that it had been normal for the past seventeen years, but there had always been a ringing bell of hope. Until a few hours ago, when four words numbed Poppy Holliday's faculties and the bell stopped tolling.

They found her remains.

Those words had resounded through her head as she drove through the misty December night to Gray Creek, Mississippi, less than two hours from the Mississippi Bureau of Investigation in Batesville, where she worked with the cold case unit and now lived. But on that chilly, late night in November when Cora had gone missing, Poppy had lived in Gray Creek. She'd been seventeen—a senior—and Cora had been fifteen, a freshman at Gray Creek High.

Poppy switched on her brights, then gripped the steering wheel tighter as the lights illuminated the dark road. But nothing illuminated her internal dark void. Tears filmed her eyes, and she blinked in rhythm with her windshield wipers. If only she could turn a switch to swish away the pain like the wiper blades cleared the tiny flecks of sleet from the windshield. Like her lashes swept away the salty tears.

She slowed as she took the sharp turn. Out here on the country back roads, hitting deer was the leading cause of death.

What or who had killed Cora?

Her sister's remains had been found along with her purse and wallet, which held Cora's student identification card.

Another round of tears—of grief mixed with fond memories—slipped down Poppy's cheeks and then she sobered as she approached the Weaverman property, which lay on the outskirts of Gray Creek. The once-thriving farm had been secluded and abandoned for years. The only evidence left was a silo and old pump house—where Cora had been for seventeen years and one month. The original house had been torn down long ago.

Earlier today, a few teenage boys had decided to play Truth or Dare, which landed one of them down the old, dried-up well in the dilapidated pump house with a rope tied around his waist and his friends egging him on. He'd gotten more than he bargained for when he discovered the remains. At least they'd had the brains to call the sheriff's office and report it.

After seventeen years of weather and time, not much would be left to identify, but a DNA test was being done, and with the purse, identification card and a few tattered remains of clothing, Poppy and her family were convinced it was Cora.

She parked at the edge of the road, her headlights spotlighting the yellow crime scene tape rattling in the unusually wintry weather for the South. Forecasters called for a white Christmas, but a lot could change in a week. Already, snow had fallen twice this month—a dusting, really. Enough to close schools but not to build snowmen or forts. Poppy and Cora had constructed a few of those when Dad had been stationed at Fort Myer in Virginia. She'd done it for Cora, who'd loved frigid temperatures. Poppy had never been a fan of weather under sixty-five degrees, but she had been a fan of besting her four older brothers in a competition.

Tack, her oldest brother, had stayed behind in Texas when the family had moved to Gray Creek to care for Grandma. He was living his dream as a Texas Ranger in the unsolved-homicide unit. Poppy was most like him, even professionally. Neither admitted their draw to cold cases had been born from Cora's disappearance. Tack had been the one to inform Poppy of the news earlier today.

Not Dad. Not Mom.

Tack had insisted Dad's reason for not calling was he didn't want to leave Mom's grieving side. But Poppy knew better.

When her family had returned to Texas the year after Cora vanished and Grandma died, Poppy stuck around and attended college at Mississippi State, then went on to the police academy, landing a job after at the Desoto County Sheriff's Office before transferring to the MBI cold case unit in Batesville. She'd loved her time at the SO, but one of her more rotten choices of getting romantically involved with Liam—a sheriff's deputy—had pushed her transfer to the MBI. Moving back to Texas instead would have been too difficult. Her brothers never blamed Poppy for Cora's death, but the accusation that pulsed behind Dad's steely eyes and

Mom's cries when Poppy was around let her know fast they did find her at fault.

And Poppy agreed.

Her remains should be at the bottom of the well. Poppy had been the rebellious daughter, jumping into potentially dangerous situations like a kid in a lake on a summer day. Poppy had been the back talker and limit pusher. Cora had been sweet and kind and obedient. The easy child. The good child. The favorite—and rightly so.

Standing in the wind, her thin red sweater doing nothing for warmth, Poppy surveyed the property. Overgrown weeds. Bare trees. The entire place reeked of decay and neglect.

Like Cora's body.

Poppy pushed her bangs from her eyes, and released past hurt and frustration without restraint. No one was here to witness the depth of grief in her sobs or the unending guilt. No matter how hard she'd worked to pay for her sins, nothing she did washed them away. Nothing washed away the shame. Not tears. Not closing other cases—and she closed more cases than anyone on her team. They called her competitive, and to some degree they were right, but with every case she solved, she expected a measure of peace for what had happened to Cora—for the part she'd played in Cora's disappearance and ultimately her death.

But peace never came. Not one ounce.

Gently, she touched the frosty plastic crime scene tape and slipped underneath into the scene that she'd observe with the eyes of a detective when the sun rose in the morning. Tonight, she was here as a broken sister who needed to be where Cora had lain all these years.

Tonight, she needed to unleash all the pain, allowing the wind to carry it away before daylight, when she would refrain from shedding tears among her colleagues as they combed the well for possible evidence connected to Cora's demise. By the time officials had made it out here tonight, it had been too dark and manpower too little to station someone to keep guard, though Poppy had pushed the issue with Sheriff Pritchard, who promised drive-bys.

Cora, did you willingly come out here that night? Did someone force you here? Were you alive when you were tossed away like trash?

As she slid down the old cinder-block walls, the smell of earth and must filled her senses. She ignored the cobwebs, spiders and rodents that would surely be inside. She wrapped her arms around her drawn-up knees and rested her chin on them.

When she thought she had no tears left, a fresh wave erupted.

It should have been her at the bottom of this well.

I'm sorry, Cora.

Sorry wasn't even close to a satisfactory response, but she whispered it each time she thought of Cora. And that was every day.

Finally, the cold seeped into her bones and she stood, retrieving her Maglite and flicking it on. She forced herself to shine the slim beam of light down the well, to inspect as much as to keep moving, keep her blood circulating to warm up. Unable to see the bottom, she shivered and spun around as a chill not associated with the temperature launched down her spine. The feeling of eyes invading her private moment raised hairs on her bare neck, and she silently listened for any sound of human movement outside the pump house.

Wind and fallen leaves blowing. Nighttime creatures hunting. But it felt like something else—someone else—was also on the prowl. Or maybe the thought of Cora's end and the terrifying scenarios accompanying the finality of her sister's life had her imagination creating shadows that weren't truly out there in the darkness.

Her phone rang and she startled at the shrill timbre. Glancing at the caller's name, she cringed. Another frigid gust in her crummy day—Rhett Wallace, unit team member and all-around Boy Scout. A stickler for rules, an overthinker and entirely too attractive for his own good—which might be the biggest annoyance to Poppy. At times, his presence was a distraction, so she managed to be careful of letting it happen often.

Answering, she didn't hide her irritation for being attracted to him. "It's almost eleven o'clock. What could you possibly need?"

Rude? Yes, but necessary.

If she lowered her carefully crafted wall of indifference toward Rhett, Poppy was terrified she'd gravitate to places she had no business going. Acting as if he meant nothing to her personally was far easier than allowing herself the possibility of exploring how she could feel about Rhett aside from being her unit partner.

She'd save his bacon, professionally. In a heartbeat. And that's as far as it would go. Besides, Poppy wasn't exactly Rhett's favorite person. The man was a pillar of patience and politeness—except where Poppy was concerned. He'd made it abundantly clear on an almost daily basis that Poppy flared his temper and ate away at his composure.

She was to Rhett what orange juice was to freshly brushed teeth.

That's the way she liked it. The way she needed it. The way it was going to be.

"Well," he said in his put-on patient tone, "I thought you might need a friend."

She wouldn't say they *weren't* friends. They were mostly friendly when they weren't bickering, and they could work well together—when the work was done Poppy's way. "I don't."

"Okay," he said with a strained voice, "the truth is I drew the short end of the stick and get to aid you in the investigation."

That sounded more like truth, but to be honest, she could use a friend. "Colt called you?" Their unit chief didn't love the idea of Poppy investigating her sister's cold case, but he also knew how much it meant to her. Not that long ago he'd reopened and investigated his best friend's unsolved homicide, and she'd reminded him of that more than once until she basically wore him down. Poppy was good at that—wearing people down. It worked to her benefit on most occasions when suspects or witnesses were hiding information.

"Yes, he told me you weren't going to back down. And since I know that stubborn tone and defiant glare—which no doubt you gave him—I get to be present to remind you that you aren't Doc Holliday, you're Poppy Holliday."

"Oh, I'm gonna be somebody's huckleberry, Rhett. Make no mistake about that," she said, referencing the iconic Wyatt Earp movie *Tombstone*—a beloved film they had in common. "I'm not backing down. No one will investigate this case like me." She wasn't called

Bulldog, in an appreciative manner, by her colleagues for nothing. "I'm going to turn over every rock—even the pebbles—and I'm going to squeeze myself into every nook and cranny. When I get done, this case is going to be closed and whoever killed my sister will rot away in a prison cell until kingdom come. No other option."

Rhett sighed. "I'm with you, Poppy." His tone bore compassion and understanding, and—complete agreement. "In every nook and cranny. Under every rock. We'll do everything you've said. With—"

"Within the legal bounds and without kicking up dust like a gun-totin' law dog. I know this. I don't want the perpetrator to get off on a technicality because I didn't go by the book. I'll go by the book." She didn't say which book. But Rhett didn't need to know that.

She could see him now, pinching the bridge of his perfectly straight nose and slowly shaking that dark-haired head of his. "I'm about fifteen minutes out from Gray Creek. I reserved a room at the B&B you're staying in. Found it odd it's not booked up with it being the week before Christmas. Owner seemed nice, though."

"She told me they blocked the week before and of Christmas because they might be traveling, but her plans fell through. When I told her why I needed to reserve a room at least through Christmas, maybe longer, she gave it to me. I can be persuasive."

Rhett snorted. "You mean a nag and whiner."

"Says you. Either way, it works." Poppy stepped outside the pump house. That cold, thorny feeling scraped her nerves again, and she surveyed the surrounding woods as the knee-high grass rustled against her legs.

"Poppy, you there?"

"Yeah," she said absently, "I'm out at the scene."

"You shouldn't be out there alone," he said.

"I'm capable of taking care of myself and not messing with evidence." She bit back a huff as she strained her eyes against the inky atmosphere.

"I didn't mean for those reasons," he murmured.

Rhett had lost a sibling when he'd been a kid too. She didn't know all the details, but he would be able to at least relate to her grief. Understand her pain to some degree. But why did it have to shake the tough foundation she'd taken years to lay? "I appreciate that," she said with less bark. "I needed to, though, you know? Alone." Surely, he'd get that too.

A beat of silence. "I do. I'll be there in less than fifteen minutes. Meet you at the B&B?"

"Sure. I'm wrapping up here anyway." They ended the call and Poppy rubbed her arms. Winter was the worst. She pocketed her cell phone and headed for her car. It was going to take more than its heater to warm her up, though.

She paused one last time and scanned the property. When it came to danger, her gut was usually on point. If someone was out there, they were well hidden in the shadows. Chances were no one was. No one knew she'd be here. But still, Poppy was on edge.

Hurrying to her car, she unlocked it, retrieved her cell from her back pocket—she'd made one too many accidental calls—and tossed it in the drink holder, then grabbed her coat. She barely had one arm inside the sleeve when a powerful force knocked her to the ground. Poppy flipped onto her back as the attacker loomed over her, his dark, heavy coat blurring his build, his knit cap covering his hair and the gray wool scarf hiding the lower half of his face.

She kicked his chest as he bent toward her, knocking him off balance and giving her a second to spring to her feet, then rush back toward her car. His footsteps crunched along the gravel at the edge of the road. As she clutched her door, something hard connected with the back of her head, throwing her vision into a fuzzy spin.

Strong arms gripped and lifted her as dots popped along her eyesight. Completely disoriented and feeling dazed, she couldn't fight. Couldn't get her bearings.

Fragments of sound invaded her ears. A car horn. A door slamming and an engine revving. A wave of nausea rose in her stomach.

Poppy rubbed her throbbing head, wet with sticky blood.

Faint Christmas music floated into the cramped space. "It's the Most Wonderful Time of the Year" reached her stuffy ears. Were they moving or was the world simply spinning?

Gravel crunched, revealing she was in the trunk of a moving car.

Moving!

Poppy's pulse slammed into overdrive. Self-Defense 101—never let an attacker place you into a vehicle. Chances of survival lessened when relocated. Where was he taking her? What was he going to do with her? Acid scorched her throat and panic set in, but she was trained. Poppy reached into her pocket for her phone but it was missing. She'd placed it in the drink holder. If only she hadn't cared about making accidental calls.

Begging her mind to think clearly, Poppy felt around the trunk, searching for a release button, but they would normally glow in the dark. No button. Older-model car. She filed that fact away and changed gears. Without newer technology, she'd have to resort to kicking out a taillight and hoping someone would see her hand waving, but she wasn't stupid. No one was out here this time of night in the middle of nowhere. Why had he been? He was either an opportunist who had seen a lone woman alone on a back road or he was at the scene in connection to Cora's murder. Poppy's gut had been right, and she'd passed it off as the heebie-jeebies.

She finagled her body to direct her foot in the right position as Andy Williams belted out being of good cheer, then geared up to kick out the taillight.

The most wonderful time of the year. Yeah, right.

The song continued with lyrics of friends coming to call. She needed a friend to come calling right now. She reared back, put some muscle into her kick and the light broke free, frigid wind rushing inside the trunk.

Poppy thrust her hand through the opening, waving frantically and hoping for a rescue. Fear skittered underneath her skin, sending a frenzied shiver through her, but she breathed deep and forced herself to gain composure. Allowing fear to run the show meant she'd make fatal mistakes. Instead, she'd use her God-given brain to work herself out of this terrorizing predicament.

Sleet and wind numbed her hands. Plan B. Using her other hand, she searched the trunk for anything she could wield as a weapon. Tire iron! She gripped it and prepared to lie in wait.

The vehicle took too many turns and twists for her to keep up with their direction. All she had to gauge time was the music. Instead of focusing on what might happen to her, she concentrated on seeing her steps to freedom. If she could envision and practice the motions in her mind, she had a better shot of success.

The car turned and slowed onto a bumpy road, which tousled her, but she kept a solid grip on her only weapon. Finally, the vehicle came to a complete stop. "It's the Most Wonderful Time of the Year" ended, informing her that she'd only traveled about two to three minutes away from the Weaverman property, but she had no clue in which direction.

Readjusting her grip due to sweaty palms, she braced herself in preparation for her fight *and* flight. The driver's side door dinged.

It was open, but no sound of footsteps. Likely he was walking on dirt or grass.

A key was inserted into the trunk and a lock clicked. Definitely an older car.

Poppy didn't give the creep time to lift the trunk fully before she sprang up, startling him, and swung the tire iron like a major-league baseball player. She nailed him in the shoulder, and he cried out in a deep voice and stumbled backward, giving her the chance to jackrabbit out of the trunk and down the dirt road filled with ruts.

She swallowed down the nausea and begged the dizziness to subside as she approached the main road. Poppy had always been a long-distance runner and was more familiar with pavement. Not taking chances on tripping and hurting herself in the woods across the highway, she picked up her pace and hauled herself down the winding, empty two-lane road. Thankfully, she had adrenaline on her side. Her only hope was outrunning the guy she'd jacked with the tire iron or some

Good Samaritan slowing down to rescue her. She hoped for the latter.

She continued to fight the nausea and dizziness as she pumped her arms, thankful for her long legs and running shoes on her feet.

Footfalls on pavement pounded behind her.

Increasing her stride, Poppy sprinted around the curve, and in the distance, salvation shined.

Rhett Wallace cracked his windows. Hot-blooded and in love with cold temperatures, he welcomed the wintry weather. It was the Southern summers that tempted him to regret choosing the snowy mountains to live and work. According to his navigation system, the old farm property was about five minutes away. He'd told Poppy he'd meet up at the B&B, but she might still be at the old Weaverman property grieving alone, and Rhett knew well that was a terrible way to mourn the loss of a loved one. He'd swing by and wait in his car in case she did need a friend—or coworker—to lean on for support.

A sibling's death was like having thousand-pound cinder blocks laid on your chest one at a time until no breathing room remained. After all these years, that weight continued to rob him of breath. He'd lost Keith two days before Christmas twenty years ago. Rhett would never get over waking up Christmas Day and seeing all of Keith's unopened gifts under the tree, which would remain that way permanently. It was the worst thing he'd ever witnessed, next to watching his big brother drown while attempting to save Rhett's life.

All because of one stupid dare from their cousin to walk across the frozen pond.

He slowed at the curve. Deer would be present and if the sleet stuck, the roads would be slick. Rhett didn't take dangerous chances anymore. No more daring or impulsive behavior.

Poppy called him an overthinker and a stiff shirt—stuffed, but the woman never got her idioms right and it drove him bonkers. But he'd rather be overly cautious and safe than sorry. That was his sole purpose in law enforcement: to save lives, not take them like he'd taken Keith's.

Whether or not she liked it, Poppy needed Rhett on this investigation. She was a wild card who needed to be reined in on occasion, and with this case being personal, Poppy would likely take unnecessary chances and risks. Colt was on vacation in the Smoky Mountains with his wife, Georgia, and his other team member, Mae Vogel-Ryland, was on her honeymoon in the Bahamas. There was no one else to be the voice of reason and caution to Poppy. So he'd suck up her ridicule and snide remarks no matter how much they got under his skin. She pretty much prided herself on the fact she could rile him up; he wasn't sure why he couldn't ignore her and shrug it off.

His phone rang and he answered through his Bluetooth.

"Hi, honey." Mom's voice rang clearly through the car speakers.

"Hey, Mom. How you and Dad doin'?"

"Good."

"Mindy?" His younger sister—by eighteen months—and her family would be settled into Mom and Dad's for the Christmas holiday. Plenty of snow would already have fallen in the East Tennessee mountains.

"Got here an hour ago. I was calling to see if you might be able to make it this year. We miss you, honey."

He missed them too. But he didn't miss the stories about Keith that caused Mom's tears or Dad's blank stare out the window. And he didn't want to be present on the anniversary of Keith's death. Didn't matter if they'd told him a million times he wasn't responsible for Keith's death, that it had been an accident. He *was* responsible. He *was* to blame. He'd been the cause.

"Sorry, Mom. I can't. My colleague is working her sister's cold case and I'm aiding the investigation."

The silence on the line crushed him; he didn't want to intentionally hurt his family, but his being there—a glaring reminder that they no longer had one of their sons—wouldn't benefit anyone.

"I understand. I'll be praying for her and her family. And I'm praying for you. I love you, Rhett."

A knot grew in his throat. "I love you too."

"Come home soon."

He would. Just not during the holidays. Most likely in the spring, when he usually visited. "I will." As he ended the call, something flashed in the road and he slammed on the brakes. He'd been careful to watch for deer.

This wasn't a deer.

A woman! Rhett squealed to a complete stop and bounded from the car as Poppy's voice reached his ears. "Poppy?" he hollered and raced toward her, as a million questions ran through his mind.

She collapsed against him and he braced her from falling, somewhat shocked at her vulnerability. Poppy was the epitome of hard-shelled and hard-nosed.

"Talk to me, Poppy." He touched the side of her hair

and noticed the blood. His heart rate kicked up. Had she been in an accident? "What's going on?"

She turned her head, looking back, and he followed her line of sight. Nothing but an empty, deserted road.

"He's gone," she mumbled and slumped against him again, her arms clinging to the back of his leather jacket. The way she melted into him sent a ripple of awareness through him. Poppy was a gorgeous woman in a no-nonsense kind of way. Never one to wear much makeup, she had naturally dark lashes and sharp hazel eyes that bordered on green depending on what she wore—eyes that were cloudy and confused at the moment.

He brushed her midnight-black bangs from her eyes; sometimes she wore them straight across her brow and sometimes to the side, blending with the rest of her hair that hung to the edge of her defined jawline.

He released her and examined her for further injuries— as a colleague and agent, not as a man scared half out of his gourd.

"Who's gone?"

She gave her head a quick shake and blinked herself out of her stupor as her long, lean body went rigid. She straightened her shoulders and put the hard-nosed mask back into place. "I was attacked at the Weaverman property and tossed in an old sedan." She relayed the details as they loaded into Rhett's Maxima and slowly drove along the road in search of her abductor. When they found the nearest access road, Rhett assumed it must be the one Poppy had been taken down. Fresh tire tracks and footprints confirmed it.

"I have a kit in the trunk. I can take an impression," Rhett said.

Poppy snorted. "Of course you do. You have a first aid kit too?"

"Actually, yes." He popped the trunk and shrugged out of his lightweight brown leather jacket, then went to work on obtaining the tire and shoe impressions. Once the casts were completed, he packed away his gear and studied Poppy. Pale and visibly shaken, but doing a moderate job of hiding it.

"Can you drive?"

She nodded.

"I'll take you back to your car, then we can get to the B&B and talk."

Poppy shivered and Rhett turned on the passenger seat warmer. Laying her head against the light leather headrest, she exhaled a long, deep breath. "Opportunist or connected to Cora's case?" she asked.

As ruffled as she was, Poppy wasn't one to not be working at all times. "I was thinking about that while making the impressions. Thing is, there's nothing out here for miles. I put the coordinates in my navigation system, thinking I might catch you. Join you in a look around." Good thing he had.

"It's the scenic way into town, but not the quickest. Why would a creep troll around out here? What normal woman would be out here this late and alone?"

Rhett smirked. "No *normal* woman would. But when have you ever been tagged as normal?"

She actually grinned and he was glad to see it, especially since her eyes were red rimmed and puffy. Evidence of crying. Rhett knew better than to comment. Besides, grief was deeply personal and he had no plans to invade those boundaries. He'd simply wanted to be available if she invited him in.

"Ha. Ha. Rhett Wallace—the stiff shirt—has jokes."

"It's stuffed shirt and you know it. I've corrected you before." He neared a bridge—a small green sign with reflective words let them know it was the Gray Creek bridge they were crossing. "Welcome to Gray Creek," he muttered.

Poppy grunted, then shifted in her seat as if surprised. "Seat warmers? Nice. I need these in my car."

"I never use them. Too hot." He shrugged. "You live in a lot of places growing up?" he asked, aware that when it came to Poppy, he didn't know much about her personal life. Only tidbits here and there from her conversations with Mae or brief conversations at their morning meetings. Nothing deep.

"Yup. Military brat…so…back to the case. Opportunist or—"

"Cora." No point pressing her for any further personal information. When Poppy was done, she was done. No skin off his teeth. "I think he was out here in connection to her case. The question is why."

Rhett had a few dark ideas, but he'd let Poppy do the speculating aloud. It would come easier from her lips than his. Besides, from what he'd read of the case file, there were few leads.

She cleared her throat and after a long moment, she spoke. "He might have been out here to remember. That makes me sick."

Killers often revisited their crime scenes for a myriad of twisted reasons. "I know. Me too."

"Or he didn't expect her to be found. He might have been double-checking to see if he'd left anything behind. The Gray Creek SO will be collecting evidence come daylight."

The crime scene tape blew in the wind as he parked behind her Acura. "Mind if I walk you to your car?"

"No, I don't mind."

They walked in silence; the sleet had stopped. Nothing seemed out of place. She peered inside. "Nothing taken. My phone's still here." She opened her console. "And my gun."

"Good. I'll follow you to the B&B and we can get a game plan in order. I'll need to know more about the case." Meaning Poppy was going to have to volunteer some personal information. She was included in Cora's victimology, whether or not she wanted to be.

The fact that he wanted to know more about her burrowed under his skin like a splinter.

Poppy clearly had a soft side.

Desiring to see it was dangerous.

TWO

Gray Creek Manor was a large yellow country house nestled into a wooded property framed by a white picket fence. Lights decked the wraparound porch, and poinsettias dotted the steps leading up to the front door, where a large wreath with a red velvet bow hung in the center. The Christmas tree, with twinkling colored lights, beckoned them inside for peace, joy and warmth. All the things Rhett had been missing out on each year by declining to go home for the holidays.

The door was unlocked and Rhett frowned. B&B or not, leaving the door unlocked, especially at this time of night, seemed foolish and left the home vulnerable, even if there were a few houses sprinkled along the road. He motioned Poppy to enter first, then he stepped in to the swirling scents of vanilla and cinnamon, reminding him of Mom's homemade snickerdoodles—his favorite. Shuffling of shoes along the hardwood met his ears before a tall, lithe woman in her late thirties or early forties appeared. Must be Delilah Cordray, the owner. He expected her to be older and, for some odd reason, plumper.

"You must be Agent Wallace. So nice to meet you.

I'm Delilah." She shook his hand. "I'll show you to your room." She paused at Poppy's condition, but Poppy waved her off and offered little information. Delilah took the hint that it wasn't her business. "Do you need anything else? Your room suffice?"

"Yes, thank you," Poppy said as they followed her up the wooden stairs.

"I put you next door to Poppy. You both have private baths. Breakfast is served from seven to eight."

Rhett switched on the light when they got to his room. A large four-poster bed, hutch, dresser and writing desk with a small antique chair graced the room. Two Christmas throw pillows had been placed on the bed and a picture of the nativity hung above the headboard. "It looks great. Thanks."

"I'll leave you two alone. There's apple cider, hot chocolate and coffee in large thermal carafes down in the dining room, along with cups, condiments and tins of cookies. Help yourself." She brushed a hair—considerably longer than Poppy's and fiery red—behind her ear and left the room.

He set his travel bag against the wall by an antique rocking chair and turned to Poppy. "Apple cider sounds pretty good." An invitation to discuss the case, or whatever might be on her mind concerning Cora.

Poppy nodded. "I'll change and meet you downstairs."

Poppy's hair was matted with blood and her clothing was dirty. "Do you need to see a doctor?"

"No. I'm fine."

Rhett didn't argue and headed downstairs to help himself to the sweets.

In the dining room, drinks and desserts covered two

old, weathered buffets that lined the back wall. One long skinny table held thermal carafes of drinks, and tiny cards with pretty writing labeled what each container held. He poured a cup of cider and lifted the lid of one of the Christmas tins. Snickerdoodles. Jackpot! By the time he'd eaten two of them and washed them down with the tart and sweet cider, Poppy entered the dining room with an accusing eye. Busted dead to rights in the cookie tin.

"I love these things."

"Me too." She grinned. "I already snarfed down two when I arrived earlier." She motioned with her head to the living room on the other side of the entryway. "It's more comfortable in there."

Rhett followed her. Poppy sat in the chair near the lit Christmas tree and he took the matching one opposite her. A table with books and a lamp put space between them, but he caught her freshly showered scent and her hair was damp. She had changed to comfortable clothing, black yoga pants and a zip-up hoodie.

He bit into his third snickerdoodle. He'd never admit it, but these might be better than Mom's. "How you feeling?" he asked.

"I'm miffed. Some jerk tried to kill me tonight. Also, I'm a little sore from being jostled and I have a headache. But I took a few ibuprofens before I came down." She shrugged as if it was no biggie, but Rhett saw through the tough exterior and false bravado. The attack earlier had rattled Poppy, and the evidence that she was still shaken was in the tremor in her hands as she squeezed her insulated paper cup.

"I called the local sheriff—Rudy Pritchard—before I came downstairs to let him know what transpired, and to persuade him to recognize that regular drive-bys aren't enough now. Someone needs to be put on duty the remainder of the night. Who cares about overtime! If Cora's killer lurked because convicting evidence could be found, then he might return." She sipped her hot chocolate and yawned.

"We can talk in the morning, Poppy, if you need to sleep." Though she might need to stay awake a little longer if she had a concussion. "I'm assuming if you truly needed a hospital, you'd go because you're sensible enough to determine that and follow through, right?" He cocked his head, and she rolled her eyes.

"I don't need to be babysat, Rhett."

Debatable.

She dodged his gaze and studied the twinkling lights on the Christmas tree. "Cora loved white lights. I think the pulsing of the colored lights bothered her. She had epilepsy."

Rhett leaned forward, resting his elbows on his knees. "I'm sorry. I imagine that could be scary at times."

"She was a champ. The golden girl. Kind and friendly. She wanted to be a scientist. I bought her a kiddie scientist kit one year for Christmas. It was just slime and test tubes." Her rich alto laugh at the memory sang in his ears, drawing a warm sensation in his gut. Rarely did Poppy laugh—a chuckle here and there, maybe, but that was it. "She was a straight and narrow kind of girl."

"Then why did she sneak out of the house?" Rhett had gone through the case file earlier when Colt sent it to him. But nothing in it gave him much more insight into Cora than adjectives describing how good and honest she was. He needed to know more. If she was normally a rule follower except for this one time—then whatever caused her to break the rule was the key to this case.

Poppy's posture stiffened, and she toyed with the sleeve of her sweater. "I don't know," she murmured.

Rhett wasn't buying it. What was she holding back? "Were you two close?" He laid his cookie on the napkin.

She nodded.

"Then why don't you know?" Pressing a colleague—especially one as tough as Poppy—wasn't his idea of fun, but in order to move forward in the investigation he had no other choice. It wasn't like she was volunteering pertinent information. "Was she acting secretive before that night? Anything happen that you can remember? She sneaked out of the house. Your parents had no idea and were shocked. But if you were close…"

Steely eyes met his. "We argued two days before she vanished. Sisters argue."

"Did you argue over the reason why you were grounded?" The file noted Poppy had been grounded that weekend, but nothing in the notes stated why. It might be important.

"It's irrelevant to the case," she said and balled the edge of her sleeve in her fist.

Rhett wasn't buying that either. "Poppy, you know good and well that everything is relevant to a case, even events and conversations that appear irrelevant."

She licked her bottom lip and cleared her throat. "I was grounded for having marijuana in my nightstand drawer. We argued over the pot. Happy? I never said I was the model teenager." She glared at him as if awaiting judgment to fall with a heavy thud. Rhett hadn't been a model teenager either. He'd been a risk taking wild card—like Poppy now. She'd receive no judgment from him.

"Happy about you having drugs? No. Happy you're being open about the events that led up to Cora's disappearance, yes." Could the marijuana and the argument over it be connected to Cora's murder? Did Poppy not think so? Being an emotionally invested family member might be blurring her investigative instincts. "What do you know about Cora's friends?" According to the files, she had been heavily involved in her youth group and science club at the high school. Detectives had interviewed her closest friends and all of the students, as well as the science club teacher, Solomon Simms. But nothing led them further in the investigation, thus running it cold.

Poppy's shoulders relaxed when the spotlight shifted to Cora's friends. "Honestly, I didn't know much. I was a senior and had my own circle of friends, but I know she adored Mr. Simms and had a crush on one of the kids in her botany/zoo class—and he was in science club. Dylan Weaverman. I told the detective that then."

Rhett had been waiting for Poppy to bring up this vital fact. Cora had a crush on Dylan. Dylan's parents owned the property that she'd been found on. According to his interview, Dylan didn't know Cora had a crush on him and he liked her—as a friend. But he didn't see her that night, and his older brother, Zack, had been his alibi. "We should start with him, don't you think? Seems like there's more to his story—and his alibi could have been lies by a big brother protecting him."

"I don't know. He wasn't the stereotypical jock. He was a nice guy and a science geek as well. But I do know she liked him. I found doodles on her notebook and she admitted he was cute and that he might like her too. But he didn't seem to know she liked him." She shrugged. "Teenage girls see what they want. An act of kindness on his part could have easily been misconstrued as romantic interest."

Or maybe Dylan wasn't the nice boy he'd pretended to be. "Now that she's been found on his family's property, he might want to change his tune. He's the only solid link. Who else might know anything? The file was pretty thin." Cora didn't socialize much—probably due to her epilepsy, but if she had meds, then she should have been able to go out and have fun with friends. "Anyone in her youth group stand out?"

"All of her friends were accounted for—on the youth trip. Mom was afraid to send Cora without having a chaperone, and with it being the holiday season, Mom had to work at the store."

"You didn't want to go? Did they not trust you to keep an eye on her?" Rhett asked and inwardly winced as Poppy's mouth hardened. "I'm not saying you were irresponsible because of the weed..."

"I was never careless with Cora. My parents expected me to protect her, and I wanted to. But I didn't want much to do with church back then. Got back into it in my early twenties after my grandma passed. It was her dying wish to see me living for the Lord—her words—and Cora would have wanted me to go."

Poppy attended church with the team, but it didn't sound like she was going because she wanted to. She kept her spiritual life as quiet as her personal life—but they intersected. Faith was deeply personal. "Did Cora want you to attend the youth retreat? Is that what you're holding back, Poppy? Guilt that you should've been on that trip but you were grounded and couldn't go?"

Abruptly standing, Poppy sniffed and grabbed her paper cup. "My parents never grounded us from Jesus. I'd made it clear I wasn't going. Cora knew it and was resigned to the fact. And my parents didn't make me go because they believed if I was resentful about it, I wouldn't keep an eye on Cora—but that's not true. I would have. I did take good care of her because I loved her. And I'm going to bed. My head hurts."

Her heart hurt too. It was there in her angry tone and cold eyes. Rhett knew that pain well. "I didn't mean to—"

"You're doing your job, Rhett." Translation—he was poking a bear. "Good night."

A knock on the front door drew their attention. Rhett frowned. "I thought Delilah didn't have any guests except us."

Poppy peeped out the front window. "It's the sheriff's SUV."

"At midnight? That can't be good." Rhett followed Poppy to the door. Poppy opened it and there stood a hulk of a man with a salt-and-pepper military cut and a short beard. His grim expression matched that of the man next to him in plain clothes—but he wore a belt with a badge and gun. Criminal Investigations Division. Detective.

Sheriff Pritchard looked at Poppy. "Dylan Weaverman is dead."

Dylan Weaverman had driven his car off the Gray Creek bridge last night some time before eleven, and was discovered by a couple of guys out spotlighting deer.

Poppy slipped on her camel-colored, double-breasted wool coat. She'd chosen thick gray pants and comfortable black boots. She checked her watch. Almost 8:00 a.m. One hour until she had to be at the Weaverman property to comb the well for possible evidence.

Poppy's gut had been in knots since Sheriff Pritchard delivered the news about Dylan Weaverman's death. No way could it be a coincidence—because now they couldn't question him about what might have actually happened seventeen years ago.

A dull ache throbbed across the back of her head, and a small knot had formed, but the nausea and dizziness had dissipated. As she opened the bedroom door, the scent of bacon and blueberry muffins wafted up the stairs, sending her stomach into a growling anticipation. She descended the stairs and found Rhett already in the dining room with a full plate of breakfast casserole, bacon, fruit and grits.

"Morning," he said as she approached. He looked fresh and put together. The man's clothes were consistently wrinkle free. He pulled off his charcoal gray dress pants and a fitted black dress shirt with style. The shirt matched his hair, but his eyes were a shade softer, like dark honey.

"Morning."

Delilah entered from the kitchen wearing a baking apron with reindeer on it. "Agent Holliday, good morning. Agent Wallace told me Rudy and Detective Teague came by last night. Awful news about Dr. Weaverman."

"You knew him?" Poppy asked as she helped herself to the casserole full of eggs, sausage, potatoes and cheese. And was everyone in the town on a first-name basis with the sheriff or was it just Delilah?

"Of course. He ran a vet practice with his brother's wife." Delilah set a fresh pan of cinnamon rolls out and Poppy snagged one, along with a few slices of bacon, but passed on the grits.

"This looks amazing," Poppy said. When Delilah bustled back into the kitchen, Poppy sat across from Rhett and grunted. Sheriff Pritchard wasn't sure what the cause of death was. It hadn't appeared to be a homicide, but he too had a sneaky suspicion foul play might have been at hand—there had been an open container of Jameson on the passenger floorboard. Was Dylan prone to drinking whiskey? The ME should know cause of death by now.

"If Dylan's death was accidental, it's too coincidental. If it was suicide, my first thought is he killed my sister. Couldn't live with it or was afraid of the consequences. He had time to conk me on the head, get away, then kill himself. But why? Why attack me, then kill himself?"

Rhett wiped his mouth with the green linen napkin. "Maybe when you escaped, he felt helpless. You kept him from finding whatever he might have been searching for, and now we're going to discover it. With drive-bys last night, he couldn't risk going back for it. Or he didn't kill her, but knew something, and when her body turned up, he had a change of heart and someone killed him to keep him quiet."

"Which means more than one person was involved in her death if that's the case." Poppy picked at her food, her appetite suddenly gone, but she needed the fuel and forced herself to take a bite.

They finished their breakfast and took Rhett's Maxima to the Weaverman property. Sheriff Pritchard,

Detective Teague—who had been with the sheriff last night—and several deputies and forensic people were on the scene.

Rudy Pritchard was in his early forties with eyes the color of dirty ice, a strong jaw covered in a thick dark beard and wide shoulders and biceps. Poppy knew military background when she saw it, and she was seeing it now. He commanded the area with confidence. His sight eventually landed on them and he motioned them over. Rudy was a man who gave orders and was clearly used to having them followed.

As Poppy approached, Detective Brad Teague waved and strode toward them. Based on appearance, he was a former athlete, with kind blue eyes. Poppy had never been one to gravitate to the nice guy, except where Rhett was concerned. He was the man who climbed oak trees to help kids rescue kittens, but just because she was pulled toward him didn't mean she had to allow gravity to do its thing. She'd dug her heels in early on and was standing firm in her spot, which was a safe distance from him.

Rudy Pritchard didn't appear to be the proverbial nice guy, and she caught his interest in her—for a flash, in those calculating eyes—but then it disappeared as quickly as another detective approached. This one was a little younger than Detective Teague, with short-cropped blond hair and a blond stubbly beard to match. He had arms like Gaston from *Beauty and the Beast*. The sheriff introduced him as Monty Banner and they all made niceties.

"Forensic team dropped into the well three minutes ago," Sheriff Pritchard said. "Lot of trash down there to wade through."

Poppy winced. Cora had been tossed down there too. Garbage. Rhett shifted his body toward her, as if trying to protect her from harsh or hurtful words. The kindness was welcome, but the way it made her feel was not. "Do we have any news from the ME about Dylan Weaverman?"

"Cause of death is blunt force trauma to the head. But the ME can't determine if it's due to nailing his head on the steering wheel—blood's on it—or if it happened prior to the crash." His jaw pulsed and he frowned. She didn't like not knowing concretely whether it was an accident, suicide or homicide.

"I'm going to investigate as if it was a homicide," Brad said. "Like Sheriff said, it's too coincidental. I'd rather waste my time and find out it was accidental or suicide than let a murderer get away with homicide."

Poppy couldn't agree more.

He flipped up the collar on his black wool coat and glanced at the swollen sky. A mix of grays with a blur of sun confirmed a dusting of snow coming before the day's end. She slipped on a pair of black leather gloves.

Bags of evidence—or simply junk—were in the hands of two young men who'd been down in the well. "We got more," one called.

"I'd like to personally go through the muck," Poppy said. "I'd know if something belonged to Cora or was relevant to her."

"You do what you need to, Agent Holliday," Sheriff Pritchard said. "You have our office's full backing. But it'll mostly be on you since we now have Dylan's case to work. If the cases intersect, Detective Teague will keep you apprised."

Small towns. Small law force. Understood.

"Do you have any other information from the ME?" Rhett asked.

Detective Teague sighed, and his breath puffed into the chilly atmosphere. "He was above the legal limit to drive, but due to your sister's case, I'm still going to investigate. Forensics is processing the vehicle. If it was foul play, we'll likely find trace evidence."

Sheriff Pritchard pointed toward the pump house. "We'll get this back to the SO, which is yours as long as you need it." He handed her a business card from his pocket. "Call me if you need anything."

She accepted, catching his subtle but personal invitation. "I'll be sure to do that."

Rhett bristled and excused himself to catch up with the forensic team. Poppy had no romantic interest in Rudy Pritchard, but keeping good lines of communication open was key to getting what she needed to solve Cora's case. Her colleague Mae would have thrown the invitation right back in his face and called it unprofessional. Well Poppy wasn't Mae.

Catching up to Rhett, she surveyed the bags of potential evidence. Cans, bottles and wrappers. Coins. This might be a waste of time. "Let's talk to Dylan's brother, Zack Weaverman. He was in my grade, but I didn't know him well. He'll know more about what kinds of things went down out here over his parents. And he'll likely know more about Dylan's situation. Was he an alcoholic? A social drinker? Was the drinking to numb the guilt over Cora? I have so many unanswered questions." Many that might never be answered now that Dylan was dead.

"And maybe you'll have time to squeeze in a date

while you're here too," Rhett said with quiet force, his accusing tone grating on Poppy's nerves.

"My personal business isn't any of yours." The audacity of Rhett to even entertain the idea that she would indulge in personal enjoyment while hunting her sister's killer was insulting.

"All I'm saying is getting involved with someone you're working with isn't smart." His cheek twitched. Leave it to Rhett to be irritated over some unspoken rule of thumb. No one knew better than Poppy how far south a romantic relationship mixed with a professional relationship could spiral. She'd transferred out of the county due to the mess, but it had worked out for the best since Poppy had wanted to investigate cold cases long term. The opening with the Mississippi Bureau of Investigation came around the time it all went sideways, and she hadn't looked back.

"Well, I'll be sure to file away that little nugget of wisdom and remind you of it when you ask me out," she barked. *Feel that sarcasm? Good.*

Rhett snorted. "You don't ever have to worry about that."

"I was being—never mind. And FYI, if you did ever change your hardheaded mind, my answer would be a confident no. Not now. Not ever."

"Well, I'll be sure to never give you one of my business cards."

She waved off Mr. Straitlaced and busied herself with asking the forensic team for information on the collected debris. After bagging and tagging, professionals filed off the property, leaving the crime scene tape in place as a glaring reminder that tragedy had occurred here.

"Hey," Rhett said as he stood next to her, his hair wind whipped and his nose tinged pink from the cold. But his voice held no ice and his gaze wasn't as chilly. This was their way, though. Bickering—sometimes heatedly—mostly over his strict rule following and his unwanted opinions on how to live by the book. Poppy never took *unnecessary* risks concerning her job. Her personal life was another matter, and it was none of his judgy beeswax.

"Hey," she echoed, no longer angry at him either. "Ready to talk to Zack Weaverman?"

"I got his address from dispatch."

They slid inside his car, the warm seats chasing away the frigid bite. She'd invest in a new car just for these bad boys. Nat King Cole's "The Christmas Song" played quietly as they reached the main highway. "Roasting chestnuts by an open fire would be fantastic right now. Or just an open fire. I can't ever seem to get warm enough in winter. It's a bone-cold kind of chill." She shivered and Rhett pointed his vents in her direction.

"Not me. I love it."

She grunted. Opposites in every way.

"Zack's interview didn't give much information seventeen years ago. Our only hope is he'll spit out something new to aid us now."

Zack Weaverman had admitted his brother and some friends occasionally used the property for hangouts, but he stated that he and Dylan had been at home all night playing video games. His parents had been out Christmas shopping and assumed the kids were in bed when they got home. Neither checked on them. So their video-game-playing alibi wasn't airtight. "You think he will?"

"I don't know. Depends on his involvement, if any. What do we know about the brothers?"

Poppy couldn't say, but siblings kept secrets with each other— and from each other. Zack and Dylan would be no different.

Rhett plugged the address into the GPS. Zack Weaverman lived on the outskirts of town on another patch of family-owned property. Poppy would like to live out in the country like this with nothing but farmland, pastures and woods as scenery.

Zack's newer brick home was sandwiched by pasture land, with horses grazing. A large white building had a separate drive to the Weaverman Vet Clinic. Beyond it was a large red horse stable. As they turned onto the road leading up to the house, Poppy low-whistled. "This is something out of a movie."

"What does Zack do for a living?" Rhett asked.

"I don't know—"

Pop!

A bullet slammed into the windshield.

Rhett swerved and the car careened through the horse fencing and barreled into the open pasture. Poppy flinched, her heart beating out of her chest. Another bullet connected with the back passenger window, shattering it.

"Get down!" Rhett hollered and hunkered behind the wheel as a third projectile was fired.

Poppy winced and shrieked as a burning sensation bit into the skin on her neck.

"I think I've been hit!"

THREE

Rhett's heart lurched into his throat at Poppy's frantic declaration.

He had to get them to safety but there was nothing but open space, making them prime targets. Blood trickled down her neck.

Another bullet blasted into the back of the car, then another.

As the shooter's intentions registered, Rhett's stomach plummeted. He was aiming for the gas tank, leaving them no choice but to exit the vehicle!

"Poppy, can you move?"

"Yeah. I don't think it was an actual bullet, but a speck of glass from the window." She had her gun in one hand and her other on the door handle, fingers trembling and fear causing her voice to quaver. "We have no covering."

God was their covering.

Quickly, he surveyed the pasture and the large round bales. "Let's aim for the closest haystack and hope for the best."

Poppy nodded, then bolted, Rhett right behind her, keeping low. Another round of shots rang out, then a sudden rush of heat propelled him forward, throwing him several feet before he landed with a teeth-rattling smack.

Poppy! Where was Poppy?

Debris from his exploding car went up in a blaze. Smoke covered the sky, and the smell of burning rubber and scorched metal singed his nose. About five feet away, Poppy lay in a crumpled heap. The taste of gasoline and soot coated his tongue, and his body protested his crawling movement toward her. His brain turned fuzzy as the reality of what Poppy's unmoving body might mean hit him.

"Poppy!" he cried, his throat raspy and raw. Finally reaching her, he lay over her to shield her from further debris and brushed hair from her filthy face, which was stained with blood. "Poppy," he said again as he felt for a pulse, relieved when he registered one. His heart rate increased, knowing she could be severely injured. He caressed her cheek and whispered her name again as he laid his brow on hers, thanking God she was at least alive.

A painful moan passed through her lips.

"Talk to me, Poppy."

She raised a weak hand and rested it on his cheek, the most tender she'd ever been with him. And it shifted places he didn't realize were even inside him. "Get off me," she muttered.

Her words finally registered and he actually laughed. He should have known she wasn't being emotional. But it had done something to him, which he couldn't deny— but he was going to do his best. "We have to get out of here," he said. "Can you move?"

"If you get off me," she said through a faint grin.

Right. He removed his protective weight from her

but remained shielding her just in case. Suddenly, she bolted upright, fear in her eyes—probably the reality of what had happened and the still-present danger. "Was it a bomb?"

"No. Strategic bullet to the gas tank."

The whir of a four-wheeler or motorcycle sounded, and a red blur headed for them. In the distance, the screech of a siren signaled that the police and ambulance had been notified.

Poppy rubbed her lower back and grimaced. "This is turning out to be the second-worst lead-up to a holiday I've ever experienced." Poppy was known to crack jokes during intense situations—it was her defense mechanism. The worst would be Cora's death. "Are you hurt?"

"Not fatally." He'd be sore for days, but nothing was broken. A man in a heavy work jacket approached on the red ATV and hopped off, first aid kit in hand. "Zack Weaverman. I own this land and called the ambulance. Are you two okay?" He knelt and did a double take. "Poppy Holliday?"

"Hey, Zack. Nice to see you again."

"You always make your entrances this grand?" he asked with a lopsided grin.

"Oh, just at Christmas."

An ambulance parked on the edge of the road and paramedics hustled over. First responders rolled onto the scene, and Rhett explained what had happened.

"You're reopening the investigation of your sister's disappearance?" Zack asked Poppy after she was tended and had declined a trip to the hospital.

"If you haven't heard," she said and rotated her right shoulder, wincing, "she's been found. In the bottom of your well."

His face told the tale. He'd heard and wasn't too happy about it.

"Any idea how she ended up there?"

Zack ran his hands through his sandy brown hair and shook his head. "Dylan wasn't out there that night. He had a ton of homework and he wasn't banking on an athletic scholarship so he made sure to keep his grades up, then we played video games until around midnight. And if you haven't heard, we lost him last night. So I don't appreciate you implying he was involved in your sister's death and sullying his good reputation and character."

Rhett had a feeling it might go down like this. "We're not implying anything, Mr. Weaverman." Rhett held out his hand and introduced himself, hoping to gain some ground they'd lost with Poppy's implied accusations. "We had hoped Dylan might have been able to tell us something he may have forgotten or didn't find important at the time. I'm sorry for your loss and hate to infringe on your time of grieving, but Cora's family is grieving, as well. And they want to know what happened to their daughter as much as you want to know what happened to Dylan."

"I do know what happened. He drank too much—per usual—and drove himself off a bridge. I tried to get him help for years, to no avail." Zack's angry expression relaxed. "Brad's investigating but he's going to see that it wasn't murder. It was an accident—or possibly suicide."

"Had he been depressed or given you reason to believe he was suicidal?" Rhett asked.

Zack sighed. "Come on, let's go up to the house and talk. I'll make coffee. Told my wife not to come down in case it was dangerous. I'll text her, have her pick us up."

Filthy and sore, they agreed. Investigating came before comfort and cleanliness. Glancing back, he sighed. Guess they'd be using Poppy's car.

As if reading his thoughts, she shrugged. "Well, if they blow up my car, I can use the insurance money to upgrade to a vehicle with seat warmers."

Rhett snorted as a white pickup truck barreled down the winding driveway. A woman with long blond hair and a concerned expression pulled up. "Everyone okay?" she asked out the driver's window.

"This is my wife, Natalie. Her vet practice is behind the house." Zack motioned them inside the truck.

Poppy studied the woman in the driver's seat. "Natalie Carpenter?"

She held up her ring finger. "It's Weaverman now. I thought that was you but I wasn't sure. Your hair's shorter and you look a little worse for the wear. No offense."

"That'll happen when you've been shot at and blown up." She got inside the truck and Rhett climbed in beside her. "I didn't realize you married Dylan's older brother." They hadn't done a workup yet on each individual initially interviewed.

"Ten years ago, come Valentine's Day," she said as she turned the truck around and aimed back toward her house. "I heard they found Cora, or who they believed to be her."

"I'm sure it is. DNA should be back soon enough."

It was nice to have not only one but two of the people they needed to interview in the same place. Natalie had been in Cora's science class and the science club. She'd stated that on the night Cora went missing, she'd been at the local library studying until nine and then was at home in bed by ten. Her parents had backed up her story, but they went to bed around the same time. If she'd sneaked out like Cora had, they'd be none the wiser.

"I'm sorry. I can't imagine how you've felt all these years," Natalie said and pulled up at her home. "Come on inside. If you want to wash your face and hands, feel free to use the mudroom," she said as they entered a large room with triple sinks and a walk-in shower. "We use this for our dogs when they get filthy, which is often. I'll be in the kitchen. Right through this door."

She left them to make themselves somewhat presentable. Poppy stood at the mirror and groaned. "Wow. I didn't think I could look this terrible."

Rhett ran his hands under the water, washing away the grime, but the smell of smoke clung to his clothing, hair and skin. "Do you think it's weird that she's working and Zack is home today? No family here. It's like Dylan didn't pass away."

Poppy splashed water on her face, rinsing away the soap and grime. "People grieve differently." She dried her face and hands and shrugged. "Good enough."

Rhett followed suit, then they entered the large farmhouse-style kitchen. From paint to cabinets to furniture, everything was white and gray. The smell of coffee brewing was like a welcome mat to his nose.

Once they were all at the table with coffee in hand, Poppy opened up the discussion. "Tell us about Dylan in the days leading up to his death. Anything that might be warning signs of depression? Drinking?" Coming at them with suicide before homicide was smart.

Zack raked a hand through his hair. "Dylan suffered from depression."

"Always or recently?"

Zack shared a look with Natalie. "Truthfully, I think

it hit him after Cora died. At least that's when it became noticeable. They were friends, you know. My parents sent him to counseling and I think it helped. He went on to college and vet school."

Rhett sipped the strong brew. "He shared a practice with you?" he asked Natalie, noticing Zack's jaw tick. Interesting.

"We attended school together and when I opened the clinic, I asked him to come on board." She glanced at Zack. "It helped us keep an eye on his drinking. He's fought the liquid battle a long time."

"It would be plausible, then, to have open liquor in his vehicle?"

She nodded. Zack looked away. "I've had to haul him out of ditches before."

Natalie clasped her husband's hand. "Zack's tried to get him help. Staged an intervention. It's gotten heated, but you can't help people who don't want help. The past two weeks, Dylan had barely even been at work."

A bender?

"Better that way," Zack mumbled.

"Dylan has come in drunk and there's been issues. No animals died or anything, but he got into it with a patient for letting her dog rip stitches out after a spay." She frowned. "It lost us business and that wasn't the first time."

So, there was turmoil between the family and the business.

"Is there anyone at all who might want to hurt him?" Poppy asked. "It's too much of a coincidence that on the night they find Cora's remains, on your family property, Dylan dies and now I can't talk to him."

Rhett had witnessed Poppy using less tact before.

Zack worked his jaw. "No one would have wanted Dylan dead. I think his drinking, the open bottle and his depression make it obvious. He was friends with Cora. The news more than likely sent him to the bottle. It was an accident…or a suicide due to depression and the inebriation."

Poppy's mouth pursed and she drummed her thumbs on the table. This line of questioning was hitting walls. He could see her wheels turning. "What do you know about marijuana being sold to freshmen back in the day? Anyone have the hookup?"

Rhett wasn't expecting it to go down this path. If Poppy had been into pot in school—been caught with it—then wouldn't she already know this? Could the drugs found in her nightstand connect to Cora?

"Kids smoked weed," Natalie said. "They always seemed to have it. No one ever asked. Why?" She rubbed her thumb along her wrist and glanced at her husband. Rhett would bank on the fact that Natalie was at this moment lying. Which meant it had to link to Cora. Otherwise, she easily could have coughed up a name with no fear of repercussions. Poppy didn't care about dealers. She cared about catching Cora's killer.

"No reason," Poppy said. She'd picked up on it too and was keeping this info close to her chest. Hopefully, she'd at least clue him in. "We'll be interviewing everyone again, doing a much more thorough investigation. Could you tell us if Ian Kirkwood, Savannah Steadman and Maya Marx still live in the area?"

Natalie and Zack exchanged a puzzled expression with one another. Zack cleared his throat. "Uh…did you not know that Savannah Steadman is married to Detective Teague?"

Brad Teague. The detective investigating Dylan Weaverman's murder.

"No," Poppy said casually. "The other two?"

"Ian Kirkwood has been back several years. Went into the army after high school. Now owns Kirkwood Equipment—farm equipment—and Maya actually works part-time for me answering phones. She also does medical coding from home," Natalie offered.

Looked like the gang stayed close over the years. Could be small-town friendships. Could be something else.

Over two hours had ticked by since Natalie Carpenter-Weaverman gave her and Rhett a ride back to the Gray Creek Sheriff's Office, where she now sat in a hard plastic chair sipping coffee that looked and tasted like tar. But she didn't care. An hour ago she'd received confirmation that the remains they'd found were Cora's. It was official.

She'd called Mom and Dad with the news and Dad had made her promise to find whoever did it and see justice served; Mom said if anyone could, it was Poppy. What Poppy had craved to hear from them both was that they loved her and no matter what, it would all be well.

In a flash she'd gone from being responsible for Cora's well-being to finding her killer. Poppy had every intention of doing that, but the added pressure only compounded an already sore heart.

She was glad Rhett had to deal with the insurance company and was briefing Colt on the investigation. She'd needed the time alone. Her phone rang.

Tackitt.

She answered her oldest brother's call. "Hey, Tack."

"I talked to Dad. How you holding up, kiddo?"

She wasn't a kiddo but that was Tack. "Working the case. Isn't that what we cold case agents do—or Texas Rangers in your case?"

"Yep. It's what we do. You need me up there to help… or be there with you?" His baritone voice softened and tears burned the backs of her eyes. She'd gotten Cora into this mess, and she'd work to right that wrong. "No, Rhett is here and you'd get in his way. I get in his way." She laughed. Rhett was all about systematic investigating. Tasks. To-do lists. Tack was too much like Poppy—on it like a grizzly, not letting up until it was finished.

"He's the straitlaced dude, right?" Tack asked.

"Yeah. His car blew up today so he's learning flexibility." Being abducted had been terrifying, but being blown into the air from searing heat was competing for the most frightful event of the past few days. Even now, her body ached and throbbed, and that was with the ibuprofen she'd taken thirty minutes ago.

"Say that again," his sharp tone cut in.

Way to slip up. Poppy gave him the lowdown.

Tack was silent, then he quietly growled. "Watch your back and be safe. Sounds like whoever—singular or plural—was behind Cora's death wants you off the case and out of the picture."

Poppy agreed, and it sent shivers down her spine, but she wasn't going to back down or let Tack know how terrified she truly felt. "I know. I'm being careful and safe. Besides, this is good news. It tells us the perpetrator is near and likely ingrained in Gray Creek's community. I don't have to go to the ends of the earth tracking him. Or them." Poppy's gut warned her that the small science club clique knew more, and that included Savannah Steadman-Teague. Wife of a detective or not—she would receive no special treatment if it came to light that she had anything to do with Cora's death.

Tack grunted. "Offer still stands. Otherwise, I'm dealing with an unsolved homicide that's driving me nuts."

"The female migrant worker on that ranch?"

"Rosa Velasquez. She's personal to me now. Anyway, call if you're in a jam."

"And you'll come riding in with your white horse and hat and Ranger badge?"

He chuckled, then his tone sobered. "I'll come as your big brother who loves you and wants you to stop blaming yourself for Cora's death."

She swallowed the hard knot in her throat. "Got work to do." Crying over the line would do about as much good as wishing someone would hold her and soothe her pain. None. Time to toughen up. She said her goodbyes and hung up as Rhett waltzed in with the cardboard box under one arm, pushing a rolling whiteboard with his other. Cora had been reduced to a case file number, a picture on a murder board.

"You good?" Rhett asked as he set the box on the table and studied her.

"Yep. Talked to my oldest brother—Tack. I told him we had the case under control."

"That we do." But his eyes held a measure of skepticism. The next two hours, they pored over the case file, reading up on the past interviews and making notes on the whiteboard while conjecturing on Dylan's method of death.

Finally, Rhett asked the question Poppy had been expecting since she'd talked to Natalie. "Okay, let's get it out there. Why did you ask Natalie Weaverman about pot? What are you not telling me? I can't help you if you don't let me."

Poppy sighed. This secret was one of her regrets, to go along with so many others. "It's true that I was grounded the night Cora sneaked out and disappeared."

"Because you'd been caught with a bag of weed." He rolled his hand in the air, signaling her to get to the point faster.

She frowned, but continued. "Right, but it wasn't mine. I'd found it in Cora's backpack two days prior. Talk about stunned. She said she was holding it for a friend who had been caught with it before. She refused to give me a name, but Cora's friends didn't do any kind of drugs."

"You believe it? That it was someone else's?"

"Yes."

Rhett leaned forward, his corded forearms on the table and exposed, causing a second of distraction as she wondered how it would feel to be swept into those powerful arms and comforted.

It was official. She was cracking up.

"You covered for her."

She wished she hadn't. Then Cora would have been grounded and might not have risked more trouble by sneaking out. She'd always been tenderhearted. All Dad had to say was he was disappointed and she'd crumble. But those words had rarely been stated to her. Cora never did disappoint.

That was Poppy's role.

She nodded. Poppy had needed to cover for her. Because it had been Poppy's snide comments and outburst that had driven her to it.

You never take chances because you're afraid to have fun. You hide behind the epilepsy. I'll never be able to say I didn't do what I wanted. But you'll always be a scaredy-cat. A daddy's girl. So quit lecturing me on the way I live my life. At least I have one.

Cora had cried, but Poppy had refused to take the words back, even if she hadn't meant them. She would regret that argument until the day she died. She never expected or hoped that Cora would take her terrible advice. But she had.

And she'd died.

It should have been Poppy.

"Let's see if we can trace the weed. Small towns. Somebody knows who dealt it and where to get it. If we can identify the seller, he or she might be able to tell us who purchased it and had Cora hold it for safekeeping." He made a note on the whiteboard. "You said you got into trouble in high school. Where did you get your marijuana from?"

Poppy sighed. "Once we moved to Gray Creek and I started spending time with Grandma, I stopped smoking it. I did drink a little and mostly did things to make my parents mad like break curfew, smoke cigarettes, talk back and date hoodlums—their words."

Rhett grinned. "Poppy Holliday talking back? I don't believe it."

His teasing tone coaxed a smile and provided a sense of comfort she desperately needed, but didn't want— not from Rhett. She was too afraid of the many tangles it would create.

"I know, right?" she joked.

His smirk sent a dip into her belly. She cleared her

throat and redirected her thoughts to the case. "What about Ian? His alibi is weak."

Rhett sifted through the pages and grunted in his typical fashion when he didn't care for something. "At *Christmas with the Kranks*. Alone. And he'd conveniently thrown away his ticket stub."

"Did the detective investigating at the time pass a photo to movie employees to try to verify?" Poppy asked.

"Nothing here noting it. No point trying to now. No one is going to remember if Ian Kirkwood saw a movie alone seventeen years ago."

True. "I want to start with him."

Sheriff Pritchard entered the room. "How are things going?"

"Like a turtle in a NASCAR race," Poppy offered with a grin.

He chuckled, then quickly sobered. "I have the medical report on Cora." He held it up. "There were several fractures perimortem. Arms. Collarbone. Ankle."

Poppy nodded. "She had epilepsy and hurt herself occasionally during seizures."

"I see. That's tough, having so many struggles to hurdle." Sheriff Pritchard sat beside Poppy. "The good news is there aren't any other fractures or breaks perimortem. There are some indicating she broke bones falling into the well, but she was already gone."

Poppy clenched her teeth and forced back tears. "Then we officially know it's homicide. The Weavermans stated they always kept the well covered. Cora didn't die and toss herself down."

"I agree." He handed her the file and softened his voice. "If you need anything…"

He gently rubbed her shoulder, then left them.

Rhett sat quietly. Waiting. She needed his patience, but it also scraped against tender places she'd thought she'd toughened up over the years. She slowly opened the report.

Skull fracture, broken ribs, broken neck… She guessed it was a mercy that Cora hadn't endured the pain and fear of plummeting down a dark, dank well. But her manner of death was inconclusive. If she'd been shot, stabbed or even hit over the head, there would likely be marks on the bones indicating so. Cora could have been suffocated, asphyxiated…even poisoned! Panic hit her gut and blood drained from her head.

"Hey…hey…" Rhett jumped up as if he instinctively knew what was going on inside her—the terrible scenarios invading her mind. He gently laid the papers in her hand on the table and hauled her to her feet.

Now she no longer wondered what it would feel like to have him draw her into his arms of his own accord. Her falling into them on the dark road didn't count.

With her head against his chest, his heart beat strong and fast. One arm secured her against him while his other soothingly stroked the side of her head, careful not to rake over her injury. "Don't allow yourself to go there, to imagine, Poppy. She's at peace now. She was at peace before she ever made it into that well."

God's mercies.

She nodded against him and allowed herself a moment of reveling in his stalwart arms, of feeling protected and completely safe. It was the closest she'd ever been to Rhett besides the night she'd been abducted. Never anything more than a high five or fist bump, or an accidental brush of their fingers passing a case file or cup of coffee.

With her head fitting perfectly in the hollow of his neck, he easily rested his chin on top—an intimate gesture, one she wanted to sink and settle into, but the longer she allowed it, the clearer she understood the consequences. She had no business wanting more, wanting this. She certainly didn't deserve it.

Cora couldn't fall into a man's arms—a man she trusted and could depend on. She couldn't love and be loved, or raise a family and enjoy happiness and a life well lived.

Poppy shouldn't have any of those things either.

Breaking from his embrace, she straightened her shoulders and cleared her throat. "I'm fine. It's all water under the creek."

Rhett gave her a pointed look. "Bridge. Water under the bridge."

He hated her idiom mix-ups and that was precisely why she used them; it kept him annoyed and at bay, which was far better than inching closer to her heart and seeping inside. That was too dangerous. Not an option. "Potato pah-tah-toe." She resumed her tough bravado, emotionally pushing him away, and retrieved the file. "I want to talk to Ian." Focus on catching Cora's killer. No distractions.

Dread filled her gut as they exited the small interview room. When the killer caught wind that he hadn't thwarted their investigation or scared them away, he'd make sure not to miss his mark next time.

FOUR

Rhett eyed Detective Brad Teague as he hunched over his desk, appearing stressed-out and in need of a good cup of coffee and some answers. Rhett had none to offer, and most likely would only add to his stress level.

Rhett leaned closer to Poppy's ear, catching a whiff of her flowery shampoo. "Mrs. Teague isn't a suspect," he reminded her. "She's only being requestioned, so don't go over there guns blazing."

Poppy shot him an irritated scowl. As they approached, Teague glanced up. "Hey, Agents, how can I help you? Or can you help me? I could use some." Hope didn't quite reach his tired blue eyes.

"Nothing new on Dylan's case?" Poppy asked.

"Not yet. We checked the shoe cast you took and compared them to the shoes Dylan was wearing at the time of death, as well as the ones we found in his home. No match. Waiting on trace evidence results from his car, but that could take weeks."

Just because they didn't find a pair of shoes didn't mean it hadn't been Dylan who'd abducted her, but Rhett wasn't a huge fan of that theory anyway.

Poppy grimaced. "Are you familiar with Cora's case?"

"Briefly, in connection to Dylan."

"We'll need to reinterview Savannah. We wanted to let you know ahead of time."

Rhett studied Brad to see if he'd reveal any indication that he knew his wife had valuable information, but his face showed nothing. "I appreciate that. She'll be happy to." He grinned. "I tried to talk to her but she didn't seem too thrilled to discuss an ex-boyfriend with her husband."

Rhett chuckled.

"Where will we find her later today?" Poppy asked.

"She's the president of the historical society. They hold an office at the Castlewood Mansion—an old Victorian on Crenshaw. Christmas is a big deal with the historical-homes tour." He gave Poppy Savannah's cell phone number. "Best to call and ask her. Her schedule's pretty flexible."

Poppy wanted to comb evidence in case something might give them a lead, then they were going to talk to Ian Kirkwood and Savannah Steadman-Teague.

"We need to find out who sold that marijuana and to whom. I think that may be key," Rhett said as they entered the evidence room.

Bags of debris littered several six-foot tables. Great.

"You might be right." Poppy tossed him a pair of gloves and slipped on a pair herself, then started her search. A million empty beer cans and bottles, along with chip bags. A few scraps of paper. Nothing stood out as they carefully searched for about thirty minutes.

"Hey," Poppy said and held up a thick silver bracelet with decorative engraving. "This might be something.

It's not Cora's, but don't you find it odd that it was down in a well with a bunch of trash?"

"Run prints. Maybe something will pop." He studied the bracelet. "Raises a new idea. A girl may have been involved or a witness to whatever happened to your sister."

Poppy snapped a photo of the bracelet using her cell phone camera.

"Someone might recognize it." She pocketed her phone. Removing the gloves, she tossed them in the trash and grabbed her light brown coat, which hung on the back of the metal chair. "Ready to talk to Ian Kirkwood?"

"Yep." He'd already filed a claim with the insurance company. "I guess I'll be hitching rides with you. And we need to get lunch."

"Cheese crackers from the vending machine don't count?" She grinned and followed him to the parking lot. At her car, Rhett paused as a crawly sensation rippled under his skin and kicked up his heart rate a notch. Scanning the parking lot, he found it empty, minus a few deputies strolling inside.

Still, he couldn't shake the eerie feeling of being watched.

"Maybe you like hanging out in the cold, but I prefer warmth." Poppy opened the driver's door then froze, following his line of sight. "Never mind," she mumbled.

"You feel it too?" he asked.

"I do now." After another beat or two they got inside her car. Poppy darted glances in the rearview as they headed west toward Ian Kirkwood's business. "We're being tailed. Black sedan. Two cars back."

Rhett adjusted the side mirror and spotted the car. "Take a left up here."

Poppy nodded and slowed at the stop sign. Kirkwood Equipment was past the sign up ahead on the right, according to her GPS. She turned left down a quiet street in an older subdivision. The car didn't follow. "You sure you were being tailed?" Rhett asked.

"I'm sure." She circled the block.

"Circle again before pulling onto the highway. He may know we caught on and could be waiting somewhere to jump back on us."

Poppy made another pass and when she turned onto the main road, there was no sign of the sedan. At Kirkwood Equipment, she parked in a spot facing the highway—baiting him. Rhett wouldn't have invited the attacker to find them so easily, but Poppy was never one to play it safe.

She held her keys in hand, watching traffic zoom by. After a few moments, she frowned and exited the car, muttering about the biting wind.

Inside, machinery and parts littered every open space. The smell of rubber and oil burned his sinuses as they approached the counter. A guy in need of acne meds and bigger arms to fill out his polo shirtsleeves flashed a toothy grin. "Help ya?" he asked.

Poppy flashed her creds, then secured them back on her belt where she kept her gun and cuffs. "We'd like to speak with Ian Kirkwood. He in?"

The young guy's eyes widened and he nodded. "He's in the back. In his office. I'll show ya."

They followed him to a narrow hallway in the back of the building. He knocked on Kirkwood's door and cracked it open. "Hey, Ian, the police are here to see you." After opening it farther, he motioned Poppy and Rhett inside the spacious office. Rhett took notice of the deer antlers covering one wall, and a gun rack on another. A stuffed turkey sat on top of his black filing cabinets.

Ian Kirkwood was a genuine outdoorsman. He stood an inch or so under Rhett's six-foot-three frame and wore flannel, jeans and hiking boots.

"How can I help you?" he asked as he motioned them to have a seat in the two standard office chairs across from his desk.

"I'm Poppy Holliday—"

"I thought maybe you were but I wasn't sure. Heard you were here investigating. You're with the Mississippi Bureau of Investigation, right?"

"I am." Word traveled fast. She wondered from whom. Poppy introduced Rhett. "We're conducting new interviews, so it's going to seem repetitious. Can you tell us what you were doing the night Cora went missing?"

He rubbed his blond bearded chin and blew a sigh from his nose. "I was at a Christmas movie—by myself. I know it seems odd for a teenager to be at a movie alone, but no one could go with me, and I'm a huge Jamie Lee Curtis fan. I wanted to be there opening weekend." He shrugged. "I saw the nine-o'clock movie, then stayed at my grandma's."

And his grandmother couldn't verify it back then because he'd said he left before she woke. What teenager woke up before a grandparent? "Could we speak with her?"

Ian's mouth curved downward. "I'm afraid not. She has Alzheimer's and is in the nursing home."

Rhett kept a cool composure but inwardly flinched. It was like this guy had thought everything through. Not that he could plan an Alzheimer's diagnosis, but his alibi was perfectly intact with no way to verify and Rhett wasn't getting a good vibe. Not at all.

"I'm sorry to hear that," Rhett replied.

Poppy leaned forward. "What do you think about Dylan's death?"

Ian cocked his head as if waiting for the punch line. It didn't come. "I think it's tragic. I'm not surprised, though."

"That he was murdered? Who would want to murder him?"

Wide eyes met Poppy's. "Murder? I thought he died from drunk driving. Heard he was found with an open bottle of whiskey."

"Brad Teague is investigating it as a murder."

"Really?" He licked his bottom lip. "Look, Dylan was a great guy but he struggled with depression and used drinking to battle it. No one would want Dylan dead. Even when he was drunk, he was a nice guy."

Was he? Natalie said he'd yelled at customers inside the vet clinic.

"Did you know Cora had a crush on Dylan?" Poppy asked, avoiding Ian's statement.

"I suspected. But Dylan was Savannah's guy and that was that. It never would have gone anywhere. And before you get any weird ideas, Savannah would never have hurt Cora if she found out she'd liked Dylan. She could be a real piece of work at times but she wasn't some deranged killer."

Poppy examined the burly guy until he squirmed, then she squinted and slapped her knee. "Okay, then. We'll get out of your hair." Handing him a business card, she said, "If you remember anything else—even if it seems irrelevant—call me. I'm not leaving any time soon." Her words carried a threat that she was far from done with Ian Kirkwood and his friends.

Mr. Kirkwood raised his right eyebrow and accepted the card. "I appreciate that. And if you're gonna be in town for a while, you should go on the Christmas boat tour." He held up a stack of flyers and handed them each one. "I got roped into helping pass these out for the chamber of commerce."

Rhett glanced at it. Seemed interesting. Poppy folded hers up. "I don't know how much free time I'll have what with an unsolved case and a possible homicide that might connect to it, but thanks." She gave him the Poppy-eye— a hard glare mixed with the sentiment that her target was an absolute idiot. She gave it to Rhett often.

In the parking lot, Rhett held up the flyer. "Dinner cruise. We gotta eat. And lunch is way overdue."

That earned him the Poppy-eye.

Gray Creek's Victorian District made up three blocks of the small downtown. Some of the homes had been turned into inns and B&Bs, some had been restored and were now lived in and a few had become historical museums.

"When does this Christmas home tour start?" Rhett asked as he slowed down and searched for the Castlewood Mansion. It was two houses down with a sign hung on the wrought iron fence. What a gorgeous place to spend the workday. Not that Poppy would prefer it. But being somewhere pretty for a day or so would be nice, and the Christmas cruise did sound promising. If only she was here under different circumstances.

A rich golden home with white ornate trim beckoned them inside. Rhett opened the door for Poppy and motioned her inside—always the gentleman, the good guy. Mr. Calm and Professional. Just once she'd like to see him lose his cool—mostly to razz him about it. How could this man who worked with the darkest part of humanity never get worked up over it? He'd never taken it too far. Never blown up on a suspect he knew was guilty of a crime. Even her chief had lost his cool a time or two.

Guess Rhett didn't have the bottled-up anger Poppy kept corked inside her. Why would he?

She inhaled cloves and cinnamon and a touch of years gone by. The house had much of the original wood and ornate crown molding, and the paintings on the walls were definitely vintage. Heels clicking along wood sounded, and Savannah Steadman-Teague appeared from the parlor looking like sunshine on a cloudy day. Fully put together down to her nail polish and matching lipstick. No wonder she'd been the "it" girl in high school. She was the face boys salivated over and girls envied.

"Poppy," Savannah said with her educated Southern belle drawl. She set her phone on a table against the wall before smothering Poppy in a genteel embrace as if they'd been friends in school. Poppy hadn't given two figs about Savannah. She'd been too busy hanging with the wild side. The side that grated on her military father's nerves and sent her mother into nervous pacing. About the only way to garner either of their attention. Unfortunately.

Poppy released herself from the overly perfumed hug and Savannah set her sights on Rhett, appreciation dancing across her face. Whatever. He was easy on the eyes. Her quick and casual appraisal ended quickly, but even so, Poppy detested the pop of green that had reared its ugly head within her chest.

Rhett's greeting was polite and professional. She didn't need to see if he'd returned his own look of appreciation. He wouldn't. Savannah was married, and Rhett was a noble man.

"Brad told me about Cora. I'm so sorry. Is there anything I can do?"

She meant casseroles or prayer. Poppy didn't necessarily need either of those things. She didn't much ask for the lending of God's ear. She'd long worn out her welcome in that department and had resigned herself to that fact—not made peace, since there was no peace. But the acceptance of a situation didn't always mean peace. More often it meant getting over it or dealing with it the best one could.

"Yes, actually." She introduced Rhett as Agent Wallace, then asked if she could question her again.

Savannah complied and motioned them to follow her to the basement. "We keep our offices down here."

"It's a gorgeous house," Poppy said.

Savannah beamed. "It really is. I feel like I'm always putting final touches on it even throughout the Christmas season. I've always wanted to live in this house. I guess I got some of my dream." She eased into her antique chair and offered them the seats across from her dainty vintage desk.

After smoothing her long golden locks, she tented her hands on the desk. "I honestly don't know any more now than I did then."

"We've found that when we question people a second time, who were children and teenagers the first time, there's always something new, something they see as adults that they didn't think important before," Poppy crossed one leg over her knee in a relaxed position, hoping to put Savannah at ease. "Tell me about Cora from personal experience and hearsay. Both could be important to helping me find a lead."

Savannah echoed what others had said. Cora was kind but they didn't know her well. Savannah was aware of the crush Cora had on Dylan.

"That didn't upset you?"

"If every girl who liked Dylan or wrote his name on her notebook upset me, I'd have been upset every single day. No point getting my feathers ruffled unless Dylan liked one back—which he never did." She said it as if it couldn't even have been a possibility, and with her looks it likely wasn't. Cora may have simply seen what she wanted to, as Poppy first suspected. She had been naive at times, especially concerning boys.

"Do you know who was selling pot to students back then?" Poppy asked.

Savannah studied Poppy as if she was testing her somehow, wondering how much Poppy already knew. Finally, she glanced at the desk, avoiding eye contact. "I'm embarrassed to admit it, but sometimes we used Dylan's property to have parties, and yes, sometimes there was alcohol and marijuana—but not always. The liquor was stolen from our parents' liquor cabinets and refrigerators, but I don't know where the drugs came from. Dylan just had them."

And he was dead. Convenient.

"Could Dylan have given some to Cora?" Poppy asked. "She told me she was keeping it for a friend."

Savannah's eyes widened for a flash before she became calm again. "No. They were in-school-only friends.

Nothing outside of class and science club. Unless she specifically asked for it—"

"She didn't. She said she was holding it for a friend."

Savannah tossed her a get-real expression. "I said the same thing when I got caught with cigarettes by my mom in eighth grade. It's the oldest one in the book."

Maybe for some. Of course, Poppy made a point of letting her parents know what she was up to. It had been the only way to gain their undivided attention; otherwise, it was spent on Cora and their concern over her health. Or her older brothers. Dad's time had been limited until he retired from the military, and if Cora wasn't being doted upon, her brothers were receiving all the attention.

Poppy had become emaciated from the lack of emotional nourishment and fed herself with nothing that would truly bring any health to her heart. She craved anything—even rants or lectures from Dad about her behavior. Cries and desperate sighs from her mother. Anything over the silence and invisibility. She blinked away the pain and guilt and refocused.

"Where would kids buy it? Surely, as a popular girl, you'd know secrets like that."

Savannah shrugged. "I don't know. I never cared how I got it, just that when I wanted it, it was available. I do regret all of that. I'd never want my own children to do the things I did."

"I understand." Poppy wasn't sure Savannah was telling the whole truth, but it was obvious she'd get no more out of the woman about where the drugs came from.

Savannah's phone rang and she held it up and apologized, then excused herself into the hallway.

"What do you think?" Rhett asked.

"What do you think?" she countered

Rhett smirked. "I find it hard to believe she wouldn't know where the drugs came from given her popularity."

"Same."

Savannah popped her head inside. "I'm sorry but I need to run down to the Roubierre House. There's a problem. Feel free to tour the mansion before you let yourself out. It's really quite beautiful, especially during the holidays. If I think of anything else, I'll be in touch."

With that, Savannah disappeared, the sound of her heels on the floor quickly receding.

Poppy sighed, then leaned over Savannah's desk, perusing the items on it.

"Don't even think about it, Poppy."

"What?" she asked innocently. "I'm simply looking at what is out in the open, and if something catches my eye…well, I can't help it."

"You're searching for clues or something that might help you with the case. If she was a diabolical killer, she wouldn't leave pertinent information on the desk or even hidden in her office, then be dumb enough to leave us alone with our curious minds."

Poppy turned up her nose, but Rhett had a point. Probably nothing here anyway. "I've never toured this house, but I always wondered what it looked like inside."

Rhett motioned with his chin toward the door. "Want to take her up on the offer? We have time and we need a chance to decide our next move."

Rhett's answer surprised her. "You don't seem like the Victorian-age admirer."

He smirked and a dimple creased his clean-shaven cheek. "I appreciate exquisite craftsmanship." He held her eye, and her insides squirmed while an emotional red flag was raised. *Warning. Warning.* Rhett wasn't one to communicate in subtext, but this sure felt like it. Or she was being an idiot because maybe she wanted a compliment from him.

"Like Savannah Teague?"

"That woman is nothing short of shallow. When her undeniable beauty fades, there'll be nothing of any substance left."

"Ah, so you're a looks-don't-matter kind of guy." Bunk. She wasn't buying it.

"No. I'm quite a fan of physical beauty, but if there's no substance beneath it, then why waste the time?" He shrugged a shoulder and raised an eyebrow. "What about you?"

"I happen to prefer the shallow end of the pool. I don't need depth to have a good time." Depth meant revealing truths and being vulnerable. No, thank you.

He moved into her personal space, and she refrained from backing up an inch. "I'm not talking about a good time. I'm talking about a lifetime. And you can play the shallow game all day long, Poppy, but I know when it comes down to the wire, you're too intelligent and deep to want someone without any substance."

Her insides pooled and she swallowed hard. How would he know this about her? Stupid observing behavior. And if he said she had depth, did that mean she was some kind of candidate for a lifetime with him? Uh…no, thank you to that too. "You don't know me at all," she murmured.

"I think maybe I do." He held her gaze, then sighed. "I'm gonna go check this place out." He left her with her thoughts, fears and something warm glowing around the outer shell of her heart.

Great. Just what she needed. To be even more attracted to the straitlaced man. She mentally stomped her foot and purposely went the opposite direction to explore the house alone.

Thick evergreen boughs draped the spiraling staircase, permeating the house with a fresh pine scent. Savannah had class and style when it came to decorations, and she'd kept it in theme with the early 1900s— elegant and charming. And yet even in all the warmth of the holidays, something cold and hollow gave Poppy the shivers.

Edging down the dark hall on the third floor, she spotted an old wooden elevator that must have been installed after the home was crafted, yet it was vintage in its own right. A typed notice was framed next to it, making tourists aware that it was not working and they shouldn't touch.

Poppy's rebellious nature itched at those words and she opened the accordion-style door and peered down into nothingness. One step inside was a doozy since the elevator cart was missing. She could see all the way down to the first floor.

Hairs on the back of her neck stood at attention, and she whirled around to see a masked figure. Before she had a chance to react, he shoved her backward.

Fear lurched into her throat as she lost balance, knowing she was in real trouble. Flailing her arms, she reached out for stability and found none.

A scream burst through her lungs as she plummeted through darkness to certain death.

FIVE

Rhett poked around, searching for the secret drawer in the old Biedermeier secretary in the third-floor library. His grandmother had owned one and shared that the craftsman put hidden compartments in all his furniture and not a single secretary was the same. That was the first time a mystery had piqued Rhett's interest. Maybe that's what drove his curiosity concerning Poppy; the woman was like a Biedermeier—unique and hiding all sorts of things about herself in secret compartments. She was a woman of grit and substance, a woman who could be studied for years, and a man would never tire of uncovering all she had to offer.

But she was also impulsive and unpredictable. For those two reasons alone, he neglected to pick up his emotional shovel. The buried treasure within Poppy Holliday would continue to be an unsolved mystery.

A goose-bump-raising shriek broke him from his thoughts and he instantly drew his weapon as he raced toward the sound of Poppy's screams—though he'd never heard her cry out in fear, he couldn't mistake her voice.

He streaked like a bullet down the large hall to an old wooden elevator where the cries had originated. He glanced down, and his heart galloped into his throat as Poppy hung by a thin rope—possibly connected to an old pulley. "Hold on, Poppy!" He quickly inventoried the elevator shaft. The rope appeared old and thread-bare. He wasn't sure what it connected to or why it was there, but using it to raise Poppy was his only shot. At three floors up, she could die if she plummeted to the hardwood floors below. She'd already fallen several feet—not quite a full floor.

"I'm going to pull this rope!" he hollered. *Lord, help me.*

"It's not steady. I can feel it giving. I—I don't have much time and there's nothing else to grab on to!"

Her frantic words sent another uptick in his pulse and sweat beaded on his forehead. How had she fallen? He holstered his gun, grabbed on to the rope and began hoisting her up, using his core and arms, the rope burning his skin as it slid through his palms, but he re-gripped and pulled with all the grit and power he had and with prayer for divine strength.

Poppy wasn't exactly petite in stature with her lean and toned muscles. When it came to fitness, she was no joke. "This would be much easier," he said through his straining, "if you were flabby." Muscle weighed more than fat.

"You can shove snickerdoodles down my throat later," she said with a little more calmness in her tone, but underneath was terror. She knew the outcome if the rope snapped. Arms burning and shaking from strain, he slowly inched backward, digging in his heels, as he lifted her up toward him, perspiration dotting his upper lip and prayer going nonstop internally.

The rope held as Poppy slowly rose to meet him.

Just a few more feet. He thought he heard a delicate whimper, but slow and steady was the only way. Yanking might break the delicate rope. "I've almost got you now, Poppy. You're doing great."

"Stop trying to talk me down," she barked. Fear and helplessness had made her vulnerable and her barking was nothing more than a defense mechanism to hang on to her pride, as if that was what mattered at the moment.

"Ah, you give such good gratitude. It's pure satisfaction," he growled under his breath and then he heard it. The straining of the old, decaying pulley.

He locked eyes with Poppy. It was like staring at his brother in the freezing waters. Wild. Terrified. Desperate.

Biceps on fire, Rhett forced a new resolve. "You're going nowhere. Hold—"

The rope snapped between Poppy's grip and Rhett's. Poppy's mouth flew open, but no words or sounds escaped. Like lightning, Rhett threw himself over, using his feet to keep him secure, and caught her fingers as the rope spiraled to the floor below.

After securing a tighter grip, he hauled her up and out of the shaft, tripping over the pile of cord on the floor, and crashed onto his back. Poppy toppled with him and landed heavily on his chest, but she was alive.

He closed his eyes and wrapped his arms around her, thankful she wasn't at the bottom of the elevator shaft, dead or bruised and broken. They lay like that a moment, stunned, silent and grateful. "You okay?" he finally said.

Poppy rose up and nodded, her eyes wet. "Thank you." She glanced down at his hands, bloody and burned from the rope. Grasping them carefully, she stroked the red marks. "Rhett," she choked out. "If you hadn't been here…on the same floor… I was pushed. By a man. The same one who abducted me, I think. Same build."

Rhett sat up. "You saw him?"

She told him how she felt his presence and turned in time to be shoved. He hadn't heard anyone running down the stairs, but then, he'd been laser focused on Poppy and her distress.

"How did he know we were here?" Had they been followed? No one knew their schedule. Unless Savannah had called or texted someone when she was out in the hallway.

"I don't know. But I imagine he's long gone now." She smoothed her hair. "I could stand to freshen up and plot the demise of whoever did this. He's seriously messed with the wrong woman. I wanted him for Cora, and now I want him for me too."

Double trouble. But why come after Poppy with such vengeance? Killing her would only add to the perpetrator's trouble. Did the killer think Poppy knew something that could expose him? If so, she'd have already said so. Unless she didn't realize she had incriminating knowledge or evidence. The only thing she'd kept close to the vest was the argument with Cora. Could it link to the culprit?

Glancing at her disheveled state and aftershock, he knew now was not the time to push. A break to freshen up sounded good. He needed to deal with his own emotions—like the ones that wanted to reach out and connect in a personal way. Protecting her in order to save her life should have been his only reason for hanging on to that rope, but he was afraid that there had been more in his resolve to save her. Something he wouldn't attempt to explore. A few minutes alone to recalibrate was in order.

Back at the B&B, Poppy turned off the engine and rested her head against the seat. "I need you to know that I can't fail in catching this guy, which means I'm going to take risks you aren't comfortable with. I don't know what they are as of now, but you need to know if they come, I'm going to take them." She continued to stare into space and raised her hand. "I won't skirt the law—I don't want anything kicked out on a technicality. But I know how you are." She turned to him. "Are you going to hinder or help?"

Desperation laced her voice and pulsed in her hazel eyes with the need to bring this killer to justice—as if her future depended on it.

The word *fail* knocked into him with a thump. Did she think she'd failed Cora? Rhett understood that line of thinking. He'd failed Keith by standing there watching in horror as the icy waters drained his life. He'd give anything to hear his laugh and be the subject of his razzing again. To feel his scalp burning as he received a brotherly noogie through Keith's knuckles.

Would he hinder or help?

"It depends on your definitions of help and hinder. Will I let you put yourself in unnecessary danger? No, Poppy. I won't do that. I almost lost you—our team, I mean, almost lost you, and I can't lie and say I wasn't afraid. I was."

Poppy nodded, but determination hardened her jaw. "And you have to understand I'm at peace with the fact that it might cost me my life to identify and catch her killer. I didn't want to die earlier because it wouldn't have brought any justice. So before you throw that in my face, it's not the same."

She didn't know what she was saying. "Hasn't your family already lost enough? Do you want to do to them all over again what it did when your sister died?"

A dejected smile came and went from her face. "My family would rather have justice and a killer behind bars. I'm going to give them that no matter what."

Rhett didn't believe her family would be okay with Poppy dying in order to put a murderer in prison, but he couldn't deny feeling, at times, that his family would have been better off if it had been Rhett underwater and not Keith.

If he was in Poppy's shoes, what would he do? He'd stay in control. Take measured steps. Practice patience as he investigated. Recklessness and impulsivity would bring disaster. He was living proof of that.

"I have no intention of being a hindrance, but I have no intention of letting you succumb to destruction in the process either. Emotion isn't going to lead this investigation. A sound mind is. You need a breather."

She opened the driver's door and a rush of wintry air swirled around them. The sky was growing grayer by the hour and the air was wet. Snow was in the forecast this evening. She closed the door without a reply and worry burrowed into Rhett's gut.

How was he going to protect some vigilante who didn't care if she lived or died? And if he attempted to hinder her, by her definition, and she shut him out, then how would he keep her safe?

Poppy sat on the edge of the bed and hung her head, breathing deep. She'd almost died, and would have if

Rhett hadn't rescued her in time. She owed him. But not enough to cave to his idea of how the investigation should go. She meant every word she'd said in the car.

But the fear of literally dangling by a thread overwhelmed her here in the privacy of her room and she allowed herself to cry for a few moments before refocusing. If she caught Cora's killer, then she could give her family peace, and maybe feel some herself by knowing she'd worked to right a wrong she was responsible for. It wouldn't bring Cora back. It wouldn't change the trajectory of her life—catching a killer didn't make up for Poppy's mistakes. It wouldn't make up for the argument that led to Cora's death, nor would it remove the black stain of guilt.

But it would give her family closure, and they deserved that at the very least.

She dried her eyes and ran a brush through her hair, then straightened the black V-neck sweater she'd changed into along with a pair of dark skinny jeans and black boots before heading downstairs to meet Rhett by the fire in the living room. He was chatting with Delilah as if nothing had happened, as if Poppy hadn't almost plunged to her death. As if he hadn't ignored his own physical pain in order to save her. Three times in a matter of days, she'd been in his arms. Three times of feeling safe and a sense of belonging, as if he was her personal and private space to run to and would always be open and welcome for her—something she'd never felt before.

Sadly, there hadn't been any space left in Mom and Dad's arms for Poppy. The ache of loneliness and sense of being unloved had moved her to jealousy, and then the shame of feeling envious over someone who struggled with a condition. She'd wondered as a kid why she hadn't been born with an ailment; she'd thought if she had, then Mom and Dad would have loved her as much too.

Poppy, you're strong and healthy. Look after your sister.

But who had looked after her?

Rhett turned as if feeling her presence in the room, and his smile made a direct impact on her emotional cocoon, unraveling the strands that had entombed everything she didn't deserve to feel or hope to embrace. He'd changed into fresh khaki pants and an olive green dress shirt that enhanced his dark good looks.

Delilah beamed, compassion in her eyes, along with a hint of sadness—Poppy was good at recognizing sadness in someone's eyes, since she saw it each day in her own. "Agent Wallace told me what happened at the Castlewood Mansion. That's terrifying. I doctored his hands for him. Do you need anything?"

A tiny sliver of jealousy heated her skin. Why did it matter if another woman had tended to Rhett's wounds? Poppy wasn't a nursemaid. She was a cold case agent. She didn't heal wounds; she took down wound inflictors.

"I'm right as rain." She lifted her chin. "Ready to get back to why we're here."

Delilah clasped her hands. "Well, good to hear. I'll leave you two." She exited the living room and scuttled down the hall.

"You're Mr. Friendly," Poppy said with more bite than she intended. Delilah Cordray was a perfectly nice and attractive woman.

"And you're Miss Frowny." He raised his eyebrows to get his point across.

"I have reason to frown." She paused and glanced at his hands again. "Let me see your hands." Just to be sure they were taken care of. He held them up and she inspected them, then held them in hers, knowing good and well she only wanted an excuse to touch him. They were red and scratched but clean. "They hurt?"

He didn't answer and she peered up into his eyes. Many men were eye level with her, and it was kind of nice to have to look up, but the intensity in his gaze unsettled her.

"No," he murmured. "Tender to the touch but not painful. Not anymore."

She choked down the boulder of emotion in her throat. "Good."

"You hungry?" he asked.

"You trying to fatten me up? Seems I recall you complaining that I wasn't flabby enough while hanging on the precipice of death." She hit him with a stern eye, but she made sure to inflect joking in her tone.

"Did I?" He feigned forgetfulness. "I don't recall."

"Taking a play from most suspects' books now? I'm disappointed." She tsked through a snicker. "Yeah. I could eat."

"I was thinking we could take that Christmas boat tour. Would you want to do that?"

She frowned again. "You asking me out on a date?" She needed to turn this swelling moment full of awareness and feelings around and quickly. "I thought we already talked about that."

He only stared at her, searching her eyes with his. Man, he had gorgeous eyes dotted with flecks of warm gold. "No," he breathed, "I'd never do that."

Well. Good. But her stomach sank.

"Thought we could get out on the water—in the fresh air. Change of scenery. Gain some new perspective." He cocked his head and a sliver of dark hair fell over his right eye. It was all she could do not to slide it out of the way.

Instead she grabbed her coat she'd left on the coat rack by the door and slid into it. "Fine, but then we're right back to the investigation."

"Okay, Poppy." He might as well have said "As you wish" like Westley from *The Princess Bride*. He was being far too agreeable.

Inside the car they discussed his insurance company and what he planned to do about a new car, then where they planned to attend church this coming Sunday. She'd gone to Faith Assembly when she'd lived here as a teenager. "I guess we can go back there." Though attending church only reminded her of her sins, and that God was disappointed in her. Still, she went for Cora and Grandma.

"Alright." Ugh. He'd been all about her and what she wanted to discuss, where she wanted to go for the last fifteen minutes. What happened to the man who rarely conversed about personal things and consistently disagreed and bickered with her? This was entirely too unlike him, and it needed to be nipped in the bud.

"Why aren't you arguing with me?"

"About where to worship? Hmm... I don't know. Could it be that I have no idea where to attend church in this town and you do, so I'm fine with that?" The annoyance returned to his voice, which was far easier to work with.

"Well, when you put it like that. Don't feel sorry for or pity me. I mean it." His grace and compassion were pointless; she was getting exactly what she deserved—reaping what she'd sown. She did not need any of his kindness.

Even if deep down...she wanted it.

"Why should I feel sorry for you?" he asked.

"Why do you ask so many questions?" she countered to summon up a superficial answer that might satisfy him.

"Why do you evade so many?"

"Fine. Because I've been abducted and attacked repeatedly."

He tossed her a nice-try expression. "That possibility comes with the job. Why would I feel sorry for something you willingly knew might happen ahead of time?"

Her secrets, shame and guilt were her own. She wasn't coughing up the truth for him or anybody. "What are you, a head doctor now?"

"Do you need one?"

Anger rose to the surface of her tongue. "That's it. I'm done talking altogether."

His amused smirk only fueled her agitated fire.

"I highly doubt that," he muttered under his breath.

"Has anyone ever told you how annoying you are?" Usually it took less than this to get under his skin and irritate him. What was going on?

"You, every single day. And I thought you were done talking."

"Besides me. And I am."

"I don't see a lot of people." He shrugged and pointed ahead. "Don't miss your turn."

"Don't tell me what to do!" But she was about to miss the turn. Jerking the wheel at the last second, she thrust him against the door and he grabbed the handle above it to brace himself and chuckled under his breath.

"Wouldn't dream of it," he said.

She huffed and whipped into the riverfront parking lot. Colored lights lit up the dock, and the boat was a sight to see. Like a floating Christmas tree decked with garland, thousands of multicolored lights twinkled and wreaths had been spaced out along the railings on both decks of the massive sternwheeler boat. Suddenly, her sour mood dissipated in the awe of the grand display.

"You think they're gonna serve fish?" Rhett asked flatly.

Poppy looked at him and laughed. "Likely."

After securing their tickets—which Rhett paid for, then refused her money—they went aboard the boat, taking in the gorgeous scenery. Poppy nestled her scarf closer to her neck and secured her gloves on her hands. The wind off the river was colder than on land, and the smell of earth and fish hit her senses, along with hints of rosemary and garlic coming from the dining room.

Inside, black-and-white checkered floors gleamed and tables for two were draped in black tablecloths. Gold hurricane lamps with white candles aglow made for romantic centerpieces. The upper dining deck had been wrapped in white lights too. The atmosphere was elegant, warm and intimate.

Rhett held her chair for her, and she bit back a remark about this not being a date. He'd never pulled her chair out before. Granted, they'd each bought one another coffees, but this was completely different. Felt all too much like a date. While she did a fair share of dating, she couldn't say any of the men were gentlemen, and that made them easy to toss aside when the feeling of companionship slipped away, leaving her empty.

Their menus lay on the table and she laughed when she read that pan-seared fish was one of the choices. She picked steak medium, and Rhett ordered his medium well. Lively conversation and laughter permeated the room. No one appeared to have a care in the world, but then she doubted anyone else had been targeted for murder or was attempting to solve a decades-old cold case.

"Have you ever been on a cruise?" Rhett asked as she surveyed the boat. The engine started and the huge paddles churned in the water, propelling them into motion down the Mississippi River.

"No. I've never been one for confinement in a big floating box for more than a few hours. Kinda creeps me out." She sipped her drink and let her taut muscles relax. For the next two hours she wouldn't be running for her life, and she planned to take advantage of the safety—for now. Because when she hit land, she wouldn't be able to let her guard down. Not like this moment. So she'd savor it. From the atmosphere to the food to the company.

"I went on a cruise the holiday after my brother passed. My parents wanted to change up tradition—start a new one. Truth is, I think they were hoping to float away from everything familiar, like presents under the tree and the open space on the mantel where Keith's stocking used to hang. The corn pudding that no one ate, but she continued to cook because Keith loved it."

Poppy related to Rhett and it connected them whether or not she liked it. "And what are your thoughts on cruises? Yay or nay?"

"I don't know. I haven't been on one since that first year. They did something different each Christmas until grandkids came along. Now it's the same old tradition."

"Minus the corn pudding?"

He paused midsip and smirked. "Minus the corn pudding." He folded his napkin and placed his water on it to absorb the condensation while her glass made rings on the tablecloth. "I probably didn't give it a fair shake. It seemed wrong having a good time on the water knowing Keith had drowned. I might be willing to try it again now. Maybe."

Before Poppy could respond, their server brought sizzling filets mignons, loaded baked potatoes and sides of asparagus smothered in hollandaise sauce.

They made small talk, which revealed more personal sides of each other. Poppy found she enjoyed the conversation. No pressure about how the night was supposed to end. Rhett was honorable. And hilarious. He'd made sarcastic and witty quips in the past, but clearly, he'd been holding back—keeping it professional at work, and they never did after-hours things just the two of them. Until now. Was this a date without them admitting it?

No. He'd never ask her out—even told her so—and she'd let him know she'd never accept if he did. But it felt like two people on a date—one that was far more committed than the kinds Poppy went on.

As the cruise ended with a round of Christmas carols accompanied by the piano on the upper level, they exited the boat. Poppy felt lighter than she had in days. Happier. Even amid the circumstances, which made no sense.

But how long would this feeling last until the guilt reached in and plucked it out with the reminder that it was Cora who should be here and happy?

SIX

Rhett didn't mind not having a rental. Poppy was a good driver when she wasn't in a foul mood. What he did mind was how he'd felt tonight when Poppy had finally lowered her gruff guard. He hadn't quite put his finger on why she kept one up; it was a piece of the mysterious puzzle that was Poppy, and he itched to put it in place. But when it had dropped, she'd freely talked about her childhood and teenage years and Cora's death. He discovered her favorite thing to do was beat her brothers at anything. That he could see one hundred percent.

They'd discussed foods, travel and how they'd been drawn into working cold cases. Rhett wanted to help provide closure for families who hadn't yet received it. He wanted peace for them, and when he could provide it, on occasion, it brought him peace as well. He had gone a little more in depth about Keith's death, but had refrained from admitting that he was to blame. Some things he simply couldn't talk about. Couldn't admit his greatest mistake and failure.

They hadn't discussed the case, but he didn't regret it. A stretch of downtime and a good meal would provide them rest and help them to think clearer come morning.

Maya Marx was left on the list to interview, though she'd probably repeat the same old story like everyone else. Could no one come up with one new thing? That was odd. Generally, after several years, people typically remembered something new or shared something they had kept hidden before, especially if they'd been teenagers and thought their parents might discipline them.

As they walked from the car to the B&B, Rhett noticed Poppy shivering. The temperature had dropped several degrees in the past two hours. And she hated the cold.

"I hate the cold," she said through chattering teeth and he chuckled.

"I know," he murmured. "Let's get you inside before you turn into a Popsicle."

Poppy's teeth chattered in reply and she stepped inside. Rhett closed the door behind them and sighed as the B&B's cozy warmth embraced him. Delilah sat with a steaming mug by the crackling fire. She glanced up with tired eyes. "I put some hot water in the carafe if you want hot chocolate or tea. Both are available."

Peppermint teased his senses and he thanked her, then helped himself to the peppermint hot chocolate. Poppy passed on the hot chocolate and dug into a tin of cookies. Guess the chocolate cake she'd chosen for dessert wasn't enough. He hadn't taken Poppy to have a sweet tooth.

Shuffling along the hall floor drew his attention, and a woman with Down syndrome entered the dining room wearing a pink robe with matching slippers;

a little stuffed gray bunny was tucked under her arm. As she caught his eye, she beamed.

"I like hot chocolate too. Delilah said I can have some."

Rhett motioned her toward the carafe. "Well, come and help yourself. I'm Rhett."

"I'm Elizabeth. Delilah calls me Beth. She's my sister. Do you have a sister?"

Rhett nodded. "I do. She's a younger sister."

"I'm a younger sister too." She retrieved an insulated cup and lifted the nozzle to release the hot water. She turned to Poppy. "You're pretty."

Poppy's cheeks reddened and shock hit Rhett's system. He'd never seen her blush. Warmth brightened her eyes and turned her completely radiant. Elizabeth was wrong. Poppy wasn't pretty—she was stunning. "Thank you. So are you. I always wanted red hair."

"You have black hair. And pretty eyes."

"Thank you. You have pretty eyes too," she returned. "I like your bunny." Elizabeth must carry it everywhere; it was old and worn.

"My mom gave me this for Christmas. Did your mom give you a bunny?"

Poppy's smiled faltered. "No," she said, "but she gave me a little brown owl. I called him Mr. Hootie and he went everywhere I went—even to first grade every single day in my backpack."

Rhett tried to picture Poppy as a little girl toting around a stuffed animal. It wasn't easy, not looking at the strong, confident woman before him now.

Mr. Hootie. Rhett smirked. She was clever even then.

"Do you still have Mr. Hootie?"

Poppy's bottom lip dipped south. "No. I'm afraid I don't."

Elizabeth laid her hand on Poppy's shoulder and stared into her eyes. "You don't have to be afraid. Jesus loves you, and He will take care of you like He takes care of me and Delilah. You'll find what you lost. He'll help you."

Poppy's eyes filled with moisture and she quickly blinked it away.

"Can I hug you?" Elizabeth asked. "Delilah says it's polite to ask first because not everyone wants a hug."

Throat bobbing, Poppy nodded. "I would definitely like a hug."

Elizabeth set her cup and bunny on the dining table and confidently wrapped her arms around Poppy. Poppy's arms embraced her softly, then tightened. The scene moved him and he fought the emotion burning the backs of his eyes. Poppy sniffed, then released her.

"Thank you," she said through a broken voice. "That was precisely what I needed."

Elizabeth flashed another toothy grin and nodded with satisfaction. "Delilah says that our hugs are God's arms around the people we hold. 'Cause we can't see Him."

Poppy inhaled through her nose as she rubbed her lips together. "Well, it's been a while since God hugged me. So thank you again." She laid her hand on her chest. "I'm going to sit by the fire."

"I see you've met Beth," Delilah said as she entered the room, then looked at Poppy. "Not much fire left, Agent Holliday. I need to bring some firewood inside."

"I can get it," Rhett said. No point sending her out in the cold when he was capable—and besides, Poppy could use a minute to herself. "I'll make sure it's out before turning in."

Delilah's face lit with gratitude and she took Beth's hand. "Thank you. Come on, hon. Let's go to bed now."

"Nice meeting you," Rhett said as Delilah and her sister padded down the hall to their private living quarters. Poppy sat on the hearth near the embers of a dying fire. Her bottom lip quivered and her eyes were squeezed shut. She looked like she might fall apart any minute. "I'd ask if you're doing okay but I know you'll just hiss or bark."

"And all this time I thought you didn't know me." She pulled the arms of her sweater over her hands and rubbed them on her thighs, but smirked, then sobered as she shook her head. "I'm not okay."

Shock split his chest. Was she going to actually open up?

"I could use a fire," she said instead. Maybe it was for the best. If she allowed him into her pain and heart-ache, he'd only want to stick around to fix it. He couldn't invest in her personally—not when she was a wild card. Mere hours ago, she'd declared if she died in the line of fire due to reckless behavior, then so be it. The thought still roiled his gut.

"Alright. Hang tight. I'll bring in firewood." After slinging on his leather jacket and shoving his hands into his gloves, he proceeded outside. Snow had dusted the brittle grass, leaving it sparkly. His breath plumed and swirled into the heavy night sky.

Poppy's car's interior light blinked on and a black shadowed figure clambered out from the passenger side. Rhett's pulse spiked. "Hey!" he hollered, drawing his weapon and heading straight for the vehicle. "Stop!"

The man raised a gun and Rhett dived to the ground as gunfire cracked. Rolling his way toward the holly bush by the mailbox, Rhett dodged another bullet and crouched behind the prickly shrub. He fired back. Listened. Footsteps crunched along the ground.

The front door opened and Poppy came running, gun in hand. "You good?" she hollered and ran past him, picking up speed as she chased the shooter across the street. She hadn't even tried to shield herself, just ran headlong into danger—like she said she would.

Rhett growled and tore after; she needed backup.

"He's getting away!" she screamed and jumped a four-foot picket fence into someone's yard. A light in side clicked on. Poppy'd have the whole town awake in no time at this rate.

Rhett caught up with her as they chased the figure through another yard. He bounded onto a picnic table and over a wooden privacy fence. Poppy didn't miss a beat, mimicking his moves, and Rhett sprinted over with her. As Rhett touched ground, the attacker turned and fired another round. Rhett tackled Poppy and tumbled with her behind a huge sweet gum tree. The woman had no sense to take cover on her own!

Another projectile tore into the bark; new lights blinked on.

Rhett held Poppy in place with quiet force. "He's waiting for you. He wants you to chase." A dog barked in the distance. "Don't be stupid."

"Let me go!" she growled as she struggled in his grip. Poppy was strong and putting up a good fight, but at the end of the day Rhett was stronger and held her against him. "He's getting away! I told you not to interfere."

"You aren't any good to Cora dead. Where's the justice in that?"

After a moment, her body relaxed in his arms and her breathing slowed. "He can't run forever, Poppy. We'll get him. But we have to be around with beating hearts to do it."

Poppy wriggled free and leaned her head against the tree. "I know. I'm sick to death of him having the upper hand."

He understood. "He broke into your car. What do you think he was looking for?"

"Who's out there?" a deep voice boomed. "I called the sheriff."

Rhett raised his hands. "I'm Agent Wallace and this is my partner, Agent Holliday. We're with the MBI, chasing a suspect. I can show you my credentials."

He and Poppy eased out and showed their badges to the sleepy-eyed man with mussed hair. He lowered his shotgun as blue lights flashed down the street.

By the time they filled out their report and returned to the B&B, neither of them cared one iota about a fire. They went straight to their rooms, where Rhett tossed and turned, unable to sleep. Someone had pilfered through Poppy's car for a reason. Did he think she had case files or some kind of incriminating evidence on hand?

A more sinister thought crossed his mind and he jumped up and raced outside in his T-shirt and sweats. Turning on his cell phone flashlight, he poked around and felt along underneath the driver's side and jiggled the interior lights. These days it wasn't hard to plant a bug. Then the killer would keep the upper hand.

Rhett pulled the lever on the glove box and instantly heard the click.

Not a bug.

With his blood turning to ice, he kicked open the passenger door, gearing up for his quick exit. He removed his hand and bolted, but it wasn't fast enough.

A burst of exploding heat thrust him three feet in the air, tossing him into a tree like a rag doll.

Poppy stared at the ceiling, the down comforter up to her chin and Beth Cordray's hug on her mind.

God's hug.

If God's hug could have been tangible, Poppy had surely felt it in the arms of Delilah's precious sister. The warmth from that embrace had seeped into hollow, cold spaces until it stretched into her soul, thawing it and coaxing it back to life. All the strength within her had been used to keep from falling to a puddle in front of everyone.

Was God hugging her? Why would He want to? She'd let Him down even before Cora's death. Surely, He was holding her charges against her. Each one was vivid in her mind, with the word *guilty* next to them.

She had just closed her eyes when a sonic boom shook the house and a flash of light appeared in the window. Poppy flew from the bed, her heart skidding into her throat as she snatched her gun, then raced downstairs in her tank top, pajama pants and bare feet. Delilah was rushing toward the living room with a crying Beth clinging to her.

Poppy froze for an instant, taking in the sight. The front windows had been shattered into glass shards, and the roof of the front porch had caved in. Pieces of shingles were scattered on the living room floor with splintered wood.

"Get her out of the house! Call 911. Now!" Poppy ordered. "Rhett!" No way he slept through that sound. Gawking outside without getting too close to the debris in her bare feet, she saw that her car was up in flames and parts had rained like a meteor shower. She raced out the back door and around the side of the house to the front yard. The fallen porch roof was now being licked by flames from blazing fragments.

If Rhett hadn't come out of his room... He hadn't been in his room.

Fear gripped her by its icy claws. "Rhett!" she called again as she scanned the yard and what was left of her vehicle. A crumpled heap near the oak tree caught her attention.

No. No, please, God, no!

She bounded across the lawn, dodging debris—stings pierced the soles of her feet, but she pressed forward until she reached Rhett and dropped to her knees. Scrapes, soot and blood stained his face. Poppy checked for a pulse. Found one. Shrill sirens rang nearby. "Rhett, can you hear me?"

He shifted, groaned, then his eyes fluttered open.

"It's okay. I'm here." She hastily examined him for further injury and broken bones. He coughed and sputtered, then winced and groaned again.

"I think I'm okay." He shuffled and winced as he shifted into an upright position.

Poppy touched the side of his face. "You're bleeding. What were you doing out here?"

He covered her hand that she hadn't withdrawn from his dirt-stained cheek. "I couldn't sleep and I thought

the attacker might not have been searching for something to remove, but to add."

"A bomb? You went bomb checking!" She huffed.
He hadn't woken her. "Talk about me going off half-
cocked. I don't recall you ever being on a bomb squad."

Rhett chuckled through the pain as first responders
pulled onto the edge of the road, away from the clut-
ter of car parts. "Well, in my defense, I wasn't searching for a bomb. I was looking for a bug. They're easy
to install, and if the killer wanted to keep up with what
we know about the case, that would be a way without
tailing us. We've been careful since our little trip to Ian
Kirkwood's business."

"Well, you got more than you bargained for. Next
time, come get me."

"Only if you return the favor. Watching someone
you—you work with run into danger isn't quite so easy,
is it?"

"I didn't even get to watch you run." She'd only seen
the aftermath and a limp heap by a tree.

"I look pretty good doin' it."

She snickered. "You look like death warmed over
right now."

He grinned through the pain. "You give the best
compliments."

"Right?" Their lighthearted banter, which was defus-
ing the tense situation, got cut short as Sheriff Pritchard
approached with paramedics. Good. She didn't want to
ponder what Rhett had intended to say before his careful
wording. And she didn't want to think about how she'd
felt seeing him lying there—thinking he might be dead.

"I guess he went for bombing over bugging—maybe
he's not as smart as you're giving him credit for." She

carefully rustled his thick hair and glanced up at Sheriff Pritchard, who was already shrugging out of his thick sheriff's jacket.

He knelt and draped it around her bare arms, the smell of his cologne—something rugged but expensive—clinging to it. "I'm glad you're only cold." He turned to Rhett. "You look worse for the wear, Agent."

"So I've been told. With less subtlety." He glanced at the warm, insulated coat wrapped around Poppy. An eyebrow rose but he didn't remark.

Paramedics examined and treated Rhett, asking a million questions.

Delilah and Beth stood with two deputies as fire-fighters doused the collapsed porch roof that had caught on fire. Thankfully, they'd gotten to it in time and the actual home hadn't gone up in flames.

Poppy raced toward them, the cuts stinging the soles of her feet. She hugged Beth, held tight and stroked her fiery red hair. "Are you hurt?"

"I was scared."

"I know. Me too, but there's nothing to be afraid of now." Except that wasn't wholly true.

If the bomb had been planted in the house or had reached farther... Poppy's bones turned to lava as a surge of protectiveness for Beth kicked into high gear. "Do you have your bunny?"

She held it up. "I always have my bunny."

"Good. Give him a big hug. He was scared too. He needs you to keep him safe. Can you do that, Beth?"

She nodded. Delilah rubbed her shoulder and mouthed a thank-you to Poppy.

"I'm sorry we've brought trouble." Poppy glanced at Beth, not wanting to go into detail and add to her fears. She was unsure about the damage to the house. No windows. A disaster in the living room. Because of her, Beth and Delilah might not be able to spend Christmas at home.

"No need to apologize. No one could have known." As Sheriff Pritchard approached, she blushed. "Rudy."

He offered a tender and possibly apologetic smile. "Delilah. You and Beth okay?"

She nodded and he patted Beth's cheek. "You sure did a good job protecting that bunny, Beth. You're very brave."

Maybe the sheriff wasn't quite a wild card, as Poppy had originally assumed. He held a tender side, but it didn't have the same effect on her as Rhett's gentleness did. "Well," she said, "I'm going to check on my partner again."

The paramedics left and Rhett stood with a bandage on the left side of his temple. A hole had been ripped in the right knee of his sweatpants. He pointed to the charred remains of her car. "We're now two for two in cars blowing up."

"And I thought that only happened in action movies. Guess we either walk or get a rental—if anyone will loan us one."

"I'll take out the insurance."

"I'm not sure it'll be enough," she teased as she leaned into Rhett, nudging him with her shoulder.

He shrugged. "I never liked your car anyway. The seats are uncomfortable and your speakers are staticky."

Poppy caught his smirk and her belly corkscrewed. "I at least have a valid excuse for buying a new car—with seat warmers."

He tugged on the fleece collar of Rudy's coat.

"Maybe you could keep this. Seems pretty warm, and he doesn't mind parting with it." His voice held a questioning tone and a slight tick of jealousy. Or was she reading too much into it?

Poppy didn't think there was more to the sheriff's kind gesture, but even if there had been, she wasn't into him. But she was freezing. Her toes were numb.

As if reading her thoughts, Rhett glanced down. "Poppy, you're gonna get frostbite. Go get some shoes before you impale your foot on metal or lose a toe."

She didn't argue and found the fire chief to make sure it was safe to go inside. Thankfully, the bomber hadn't had any intention of blowing up anything more than the car and whoever was inside. The house might smell like smoke for a few days but the structure was sound, and once the porch was rebuilt, the mess cleaned and windows fixed, it would be as if nothing had exploded.

Inside, she doctored her feet with a first aid kit Delilah had provided. They would be sore and tender for a few days, but she could wear thicker socks for extra cushion.

Needing a few minutes to process, she plunked onto the bed and fell backward, exhausted. She was a roller coaster of emotions. Rhett had nearly died. He should have known better than to go out there alone. He was smarter than that. So why did he? Why be impulsive when he always chose the safe route? No wonder he got his dander up when Poppy did things like this. She was irritated, angry, frightened and frantic. But she was also thankful and grateful he was still alive.

A knock sounded. "Can I come in?" Rhett asked.

Poppy sat up and scooted to the edge of the bed, then granted him permission. "How are your feet?"

"Sore."

He sat beside her. "Detective Teague is here and that other detective. I can't remember his name."

"Monty Banner."

"Right." He perused her room. "Where's the sheriff's coat?"

And the team called her the bulldog. "I gave it to Delilah to return to him."

"I see."

She wasn't sure he did. "You scared me." There, she said it, though uncertain why. It kind of bubbled out without permission, but it was the truth. "I mean, I've been afraid. A killer keeps coming after me. I'd be remiss not to admit some fear. But my need to solve Cora's murder is greater. But tonight..." That wasn't a different kind of fear. The kind she'd only felt once before, when Cora never came home. And while she wasn't ready to discuss the root of it, she wanted him to know that... Well, she wasn't sure what she wanted him to know.

"I'm sorry," he murmured as his shoulder brushed hers. He'd changed into clean sweats and a Vols sweatshirt. She'd only come to know he loved the Volunteers when they'd worked the football corruption case last fall. There was so much she didn't know about Rhett and wanted to, but wouldn't inquire. "I'm not sure what I was thinking."

"Neither am I. You always consider long and hard before going into something. If you had given it more thought, the idea it could have been a bomb would have crossed your mind and the Rhett I know would have called a bomb squad to check. That wasn't like you." Maybe that's what unsettled her—he was out of the ordinary. Predictable Rhett was easy to maneuver around and never crossed lines. Now, what lines might he cross? And how would she keep up her guard if he wasn't the consistent and constant Rhett?

"I know," he breathed and arrested her with his eyes, searching as if she would have the reasons for his impulsive decision. "I... You scare me, Poppy."

Was that his answer to his reckless decision? He'd done it for her or because of her? What was his meaning? If she didn't look away, she might find the answer in his eyes and she dared not ask for fear he'd clarify—and they could not go beyond colleagues who sometimes got along because then there'd be no going back and it would end disastrously. And end it would. She sabotaged her relationships—if they could even be called that. Rhett was no typical guy. He didn't deserve to be hurt, and she would hurt him. Then where would that leave them professionally?

If only her heart and her head would get on the same stupid page! "It's probably best that way," she whispered. If he was scared of her, he'd steer clear of her and then she wouldn't have to worry about making a gargantuan mistake.

"Maybe." He brushed a bang from her eye, sending her pulse into a frenzied skitter. "Probably."

"You're not a risk taker." Except tonight he had been. Her stomach dipped.

"No," he breathed as his head slowly descended toward her lips. "No, I'm not."

Guess he couldn't get his head and heart on the same page either.

As his lips touched hers, a knock jerked them from

the crackling moment, saving them from going to a place they couldn't get back from. And still she regretted the interruption. "Come in," Poppy said through a choked voice and stood up, giving her some distance from Rhett and his inviting lips.

Detective Monty Banner opened the door, looming in the door frame. He clearly spent his free time at the gym—he was attractive, with the right amount of stubble and swagger. "Sorry to interrupt, but I need to ask y'all a few questions."

"Where's Detective Teague?" Rhett asked.

"Questioning Delilah and neighbors." He perched on an old ladder back chair, the seat creaking at the strain of his weight. "Sheriff called in a construction company to secure the breached area. Everyone can remain in the home. So let's move on to more-pressing things. Like what happened."

Rhett explained what transpired prior to the explosion and Poppy picked up from there, since Rhett had been knocked unconscious.

Monty wrote it all on his legal pad. "Bomb appears homemade. Any online tutorial could guide someone. We found the front of an egg timer. Nothing too complicated. But I worked for the Memphis Police Department bomb unit for six years. Thought coming back home would mean never seeing a bomb again. Surprise." His laugh was deep and amusing, and there was ironic humor in his eyes. "That's all I need for now. Get some shut-eye. Sheriff put a unit on the house, especially since there's civilians inside."

Monty closed the door behind them, leaving an awkwardness hovering over them. The moment for a kiss was gone, but the shocking knowledge they'd almost let it happen remained, and quite frankly, Poppy didn't have it in her to discuss it. "I think we should consider finding somewhere else to stay so as not to put anyone in further danger."

Rhett ran a hand through his hair. "Where? We'd have to find something to rent that was private. Know of any place?"

"There's a campground with cabins a few miles south of the Weaverman property. I can check availability. If Beth and Delilah are harmed because of me... I'd never forgive myself." She wouldn't be responsible for any more deaths.

Rhett stood. "I understand. But we have to be prepared that we might not find anywhere else. We'll take more precautions." He scratched the back of his neck. "Should we...uh...talk about—"

"Nothing to talk about. It was a highly emotional moment. That's all. It could have been Detective Banner or Sheriff Pritchard. I may have kissed either of them given the circumstances."

The last thing she wanted to discuss was her feelings—her extremely conflicted feelings—and as she made eye contact, the pain she'd intended to inflict hit its mark. It was there in the flash of hurt and the tick in his jaw.

"But *I* wouldn't have kissed just anyone."

"That sounds like a personal problem and talking about it to me is unnecessary. Work out your own feelings on your own time." It crushed her to speak such icy words, but she had a wall to rebuild, so she trained her line of sight right above his eyes for fear if she gazed into that warmth and gentleness, she'd desperately want to be pursued and loved by a good, honest man. He'd see her false bravado and maybe even glimpse her emotional struggle concerning her feelings for him, and it would be over for them both.

Rhett squared his shoulders and inhaled sharply through his nose. "I was going to say that even if a kernel of something was there fueling that moment, I'm sorry. I don't date colleagues and I especially don't date loose cannons. But I won't pretend that I'm not attracted to you. You're a beautiful, smart woman—most of the time you're smart." He actually smirked. "And that was obviously what led the charge thanks to heightened emotions that come with near-death experiences. You're right on that account. So that's that. You're free to run off now and kiss any man that crosses your path."

He didn't slam the door. Didn't raise his voice.

She didn't want to kiss anyone except him. And he didn't see her as anything other than an intelligent but pretty face. No, he didn't want her and her loose-cannon ways.

SEVEN

Rhett stared at the collected bomb debris from Saturday night. Detective Teague's canvassing had gotten zero answers. All they had were suspects, blown-up vehicles and sore bodies. Everyone felt the frustration. Now he sipped lukewarm coffee made by a deputy who didn't know when to stop with the scooping. A spoon could stand up straight in this stuff.

Typical Monday at the sheriff's office. Slow but rushed. It was only 10:00 a.m. but it felt like five o'clock.

Yesterday after church and lunch, Poppy had called the campground to check on a vacant cabin for the rest of their stay. Rhett wasn't keen on spending the remainder of the investigation in that kind of close proximity with her. Alone. No buffers. No barriers. Not because he'd kiss her again, but after their terse conversation Saturday night, he needed space to get his head back in the game and on track. Poppy had been right—it wasn't like him to allow emotions to guide his decisions. He never made quick or impulsive ones. But Poppy had a pull on him, which was terrifying.

He hadn't meant to hurt her feelings—if he even had—when he'd declared he'd never date a loose cannon like her, but she'd drawn first blood when she'd admitted she would have kissed any man who had been sitting there beside her. He wished those words wouldn't have cut, but they had, and his ego took a nice hit too.

Better that it worked out the way it did anyway. Had she admitted there was something there and made a move to finish what they'd started before Detective Banner had become the proverbial bell, it would have meant even greater turmoil for Rhett. He could only hope there would be no vacant cabins and he wouldn't have to suffer being confined with Poppy. She'd left a message and surely the campground manager would call by today.

Poppy entered the evidence room scowling. Dressed in black pants and a black-and-white-striped dress shirt that fit trim at her slender waist, she held a cup of a coffee. "The coffee is rank, I know."

"It's not the coffee—though you're right. We're stuck at the B&B. No cabins available."

A slight breath of relief escaped his lungs and created some space in his chest. He didn't want to put anyone at risk either, but they were on high alert now and would take more precautions. Plus, Delilah had insisted they stay. The woman had a lot of class and grace.

"The bright side is, our rental has seat warmers and that makes me happy." She sipped her sludge.

She'd been going on about that since yesterday when they picked a midsize sedan. "You update the chief yet?"

That garnered a grin. "Colt asked if we blew up each other's cars. Me to be spiteful and you to retaliate." Her grin morphed into the Poppy-eye. "I told him you'd never do something so unpredictable or loose-cannon-like."

Okay, so that statement had affected her. "I wasn't trying to insult you."

"I know. I am both of those things." She shrugged as if it simply was what it was. "Maya Marx. Let's go talk to her. She's at the vet clinic today."

"You want to drive or me?"

"Feel free." She tossed him the keys.

Weaverman Vet Clinic wasn't all that busy. Pet dander and stringent floor cleaner tickled and burned Rhett's nose. A Yellow Lab sat by his owner quietly while a Yorkie in a huge pink bow yapped away while her owner ignored the shrill barks.

A woman wearing scrubs, with frizzy hair and lips that revealed many years of smoking, eyed him and Poppy. He showed her his credentials and explained why they were there.

"Maya is actually on a fifteen-minute break. Follow me." She led them through a door to a large room with kennels and steel tables. Dogs barked and whined. Poor pups. Rhett did a double-take as a huge turtle poked its head from its shell.

Maya Marx stood in the break room, the side door open to the outside while she engaged in a tense conversation with Detective Monty Banner. Well, that was interesting. Rhett cleared his throat and Maya swung her attention to them. She was short and petite with a severe blond ponytail and rich brown eyes.

Detective Banner's cheeks reddened. "Agents," he said and introduced them to Maya, then made a quick exit. What were they discussing? She wasn't a suspect in the attempts on their lives, but she did connect to the cold case, which connected to Rhett's and Poppy's lives being threatened. She'd been in Cora's science class and club, and she had been BFFs with Savannah Steadman-Teague and Natalie Carpenter-Weaverman. And ran with Dylan and Ian.

"How can I help you?" She closed the heavy metal door and a whiff of stale cigarettes reached his nostrils. Cheap cigarettes lay by a box of doughnuts.

Poppy shoved her hands into her coat pockets. "You and Detective Banner seeing each other?"

"For a few months, but I hardly think that's why you're here." She sat in the plastic chair and laid a hand over her pack of cigarettes.

"You're right. We're interviewing past friends, club members and classmates of Cora's, seeing if any new information comes to light. Can you go over that night for us again? And don't leave out the fact that Dylan had a crush on Cora. One of our earlier interviews happened to remember that piece of information after all these years."

Rhett kept a straight face at Poppy's stretch. It wasn't illegal to bend the truth, and Poppy was bending it pretty far. No one had veered outside of their old story, but if Maya thought one of them had, she might offer up information she'd have otherwise withheld. Rhett was never a fan of this tactic, and Poppy knew it.

Maya toyed with the plastic cigarette packaging. "I knew Cora liked Dylan. And yes, Dylan was into her. I saw them passing notes in science club a few times and he carried her books to the next class—but it wasn't going to go anywhere."

And it worked.

"Because of Savannah?" Poppy asked.

"Because it was a crush, and Dylan was ultimately devoted to Savannah. Savannah would never have harmed Cora."

"What about Ian Kirkwood?" Rhett asked. "Could he have killed someone?"

She frowned. "Doubtful."

"His alibi is lame. Movies alone? Does that sound like something he would have done?" Rhett asked, hoping for any scent to hunt.

Maya's cheeks reddened. "No. I doubt he'd have gone to a movie alone, but he was a major Jamie Lee Curtis fan."

"Who was dealing pot back then? I know about the marijuana Cora had too."

Maya snorted. "You want the dealer? Easy enough. Linden Saddler. He was generally at the Pet Company off Highway 10. He owns the place now. We're his vet for animals that get sick at the store."

Another connection Natalie was keeping close. Now they might be getting somewhere. "He ever sell to you?"

"No. I never bought drugs." She didn't say she never did them.

They thanked her for her time and within fifteen minutes pulled into the Pet Company parking lot.

"Let's hope this guy remembers who he dealt to back then, but if he's continued to sell over the years, he'll likely not talk." Rhett unbuckled his seat belt.

"I don't care what he's doing now because at the moment he's our only lead." Poppy slammed the car door and flipped up the collar on her coat. The snow and sleet had let up, but the slate sky was growing heavier by the hour. Snow would fall again tonight.

Inside, animals rattled cages, puppies barked and

Rhett frowned. "I'm not a fan of puppy mills. And most pet stores get their animals from them and then jack up the price. That ought to be a crime."

Poppy smirked. "I didn't realize you were such an animal activist." Birds squawked and chirped. A whole row of mice and hamsters ran in hamster wheels. Poppy turned her nose up. "Though I do agree."

Now Rhett chuckled but didn't say anything. A teenager with more acne than hair on his head noticed them and waved. "If you need any help, let me know."

"We're looking for Mr. Saddler. He in?"

"Yes, ma'am. I'll go get him." The guy rushed through the aisles and to the back of the store. A few moments passed and a muscular man with eighties hairband hair and a rock T-shirt came tagging along behind the teenager.

"I'm Linden Saddler. Can I help you?" He kept his eyes on Poppy. Like the teenager. Like most of the male species. Rhett never faulted them for it; he was clearly a sucker too.

"I'm Agent Holliday and this is Agent Wallace. We're investigating the murder of Cora Holliday—yes, she's a relation."

"I heard about that. Sorry for your loss. We can talk in my office. Follow me back."

His office looked more like a boy's bedroom full of posters from bands who had fallen from their prime.

"I love eighties rock."

"I wouldn't have guessed," Poppy teased and Saddler responded with a fat grin. "Look, I'm gonna be straight up with you. I'm not interested in what you might do on the side. Nor am I interested in bringing any charges against you for the past—unless you murdered my sister—so you can be candid with me."

"I didn't kill anyone. Can't get any more candid than that." He tented his fingers on his messy desk.

"Then let's keep rolling with that. Tell me who you sold pot to back then. Cora had a bag and said she was holding it for a friend. I think that friend might have had something to do with her death. It's at the very least a lead for me. You say you're sorry for my loss? Help me find the killer. If it wasn't you, then you have nothing to lose and everything to gain—my gratitude for one." She left it hanging as if there might be more reward for him.

He leaned his head back against his chair. "I don't sell drugs anymore. I did sell weed on the side and used it to save up to buy this place."

"You ever deal to Dylan Weaverman, Ian Kirkwood, Savannah Steadman, Maya Marx or Natalie Carpenter?"

"I sold to all of them except Maya."

"Did you sell to any of them the week or so before Cora went missing? It would have been the week before Thanksgiving," Poppy said.

It was a long shot but who knew. Maybe he kept a record or had a keen mind.

Linden tossed his hands in the air. "That was a long time ago. What I can tell you is that if your sister was on the bad side of mean girl Savannah Steadman and her loyal sidekicks, then if one of them gave her drugs it wasn't to befriend her but to get her in trouble. And if your sister did somehow manage to wiggle her way into their circle, then she was as catty as they were."

Poppy glanced at Rhett, then back to Linden. "Cora

wasn't popular. Her only friends were in youth group. She didn't have a mean bone in her body."

"Then she was a target or being used. Those chicks were ruthless. I seen 'em in action at parties out at the W. That's what they all called the Weaverman property back then."

"Did you go out there the night Cora went missing?"

"Nah." He tapped his pen on the desk. "No party. I'd have heard if there was. Besides, if there had been a big shindig, someone would have seen something and come forward, don't you think?"

"Maybe. Except if a bunch of kids were out there drinking and doing drugs, they'd want to keep it quiet for fear of getting in trouble by parents." She tapped her index finger on her bottom lip. "You remember any of these other girls that were bullied by this mean-girl group? Now that they're older, they might be willing to share their stories, give me some insight. Enjoy a little payback."

He chuckled. "Unless they bought weed from me, I don't know names. Sorry."

"If you remember, call me." She handed him her card and they started for the door.

"Wait. Yes, I do. Her brother went off to the military and moved back home not too long ago. Works for the sheriff now. Detective or something."

"Monty Banner?"

"Banner. Yeah, that's it."

Poppy's eyebrows rose. She must be thinking what Rhett was. Why would Monty Banner be dating a girl who had bullied his sister in high school? And did it have anything to do with not divulging the information to them?

* * *

Poppy plopped into the rental car seat, her mind buzzing with the new information and where it could lead—if anywhere. "I don't remember anything about those girls being bullies. But then, I didn't pay much attention to what didn't personally affect me. I did, however, look out for Cora and she never once said anyone was messing with her." She rubbed her temples. "What if Linden was trying to throw suspicion on anyone but himself?" If Cora had taken her terrible advice, purchased marijuana from Linden then regretted it, if Linden had caught wind she might rat him out, he may have killed her.

"We can continue to look into him. See if he has any priors. In the meantime, let's run down this lead." She called Sheriff Pritchard, put him on speaker and relayed the new update. "Can you tell us where we might find Banner's sister?"

"Candy. Works part-time at the library and she's a photographer."

"Thanks. And if you wouldn't let Monty know, that would be great."

"Won't say a word. But Monty is a stand-up guy. A war hero."

"Either way." She hurriedly ended the call. "Let's try the library first."

The small library was across town, behind the courthouse. The square was in full swing with shoppers. The scent of grilled beef wafted on the air and Poppy's stomach rumbled. It had been a few hours since she'd choked down a stale doughnut and lukewarm coffee.

The railings on the concrete stairs leading to the library were lined with garland and silver bells. Bright

Get up to 4
FREE FABULOUS BOOKS
You Love!

To thank you for being a loyal reader we'd like to send you up to 4 FREE BOOKS, absolutely free.

Just write "YES" on the Loyal Reader Voucher and we'll send you up to 4 Free Books and Free Mystery Gifts, altogether worth over $20, as a way of saying thank you for being a loyal reader.

Try **Love Inspired® Romance Larger-Print** books and fall in love with inspirational romances that take you on an uplifting journey of faith, forgiveness and hope.

Try **Love Inspired® Suspense Larger-Print** books where courage and optimism unite in stories of faith and love in the face of danger.

Or **TRY BOTH!**

We are so glad you love the books as much as we do and can't wait to send you great new books.

So don't miss out, return your Loyal Reader Voucher Today!

Pam Powers

LOYAL READER
FREE BOOKS VOUCHER

▼ DETACH AND MAIL CARD TODAY! ▼

YES! I Love Reading, please send me up to 4 FREE BOOKS and Free Mystery Gifts from the series I select.

Just write in "YES" on the dotted line below then return this card today and we'll send your free books & gifts asap!

Which do you prefer?

| ☐ **Love Inspired®**
Romance
Larger-Print
122/322 IDL GRJD | ☐ **Love Inspired®**
Suspense
Larger-Print
107/307 IDL GRJD | ☐ **BOTH**
122/322 & 107/307
IDL GRJP |

FIRST NAME | LAST NAME

ADDRESS

APT.# | CITY

STATE/PROV. | ZIP/POSTAL CODE

EMAIL ☐ Please check this box if you would like to receive newsletters and promotional emails from Harlequin Enterprises ULC and its affiliates. You can unsubscribe anytime.

LI/SLI-520-LR21

BUSINESS REPLY MAIL
FIRST-CLASS MAIL   PERMIT NO. 717   BUFFALO, NY

POSTAGE WILL BE PAID BY ADDRESSEE

HARLEQUIN READER SERVICE
PO BOX 1341
BUFFALO NY 14240-8571

NO POSTAGE
NECESSARY
IF MAILED
IN THE
UNITED STATES

green wreaths with red velvet bows graced the glass doors. Inside the library foyer, they were met with a colorfully lit Christmas tree made from books and stacked canned goods nearby for a Christmas food drive. Red and green paper lanterns hung from the ceiling tiles, and red and green lights draped the tops of the bookshelves.

"You go see if you can find Candy Banner, and I'm going to see if the reference section carries old yearbooks. Maybe we can peruse the annuals. Pictures say a thousand words or something like that, right? You can find out a lot about social life from a high school yearbook," Rhett said.

Poppy didn't disagree; they were running out of options. "Have at it." She strolled to the information desk and was greeted by an older woman wearing a Mrs. Claus costume.

"Can I help you?" she asked.

"I'm looking for Candy Banner. Is she in today?"

"I'm afraid not. She's working at Santa's Village as a photographer. She takes the loveliest pictures. She only works here part-time."

"Thanks for your time." She hurried back to the reference section to see Rhett's mile-wide grin.

"What are you doing? Dare I ask?" Poppy asked.

"Research," he mused.

Poppy caught the headline. "Why are you in the seniors' section when you know good and well…" Realization dawned. "Hey! Get out of my senior section."

Rhett low-whistled. "You look nothing like this now."

"Well, times have changed." Back then her hair had hung past her shoulders, and she'd been more lithe than lean muscled due to running but no weight training. And her eye liner was more pronounced. Lips cherry red. It was kind of her thing. He closed the book and grinned at her with smug satisfaction.

"What?" she huffed.

"Nothing. I like you better now."

She rolled her eyes. "Candy Banner works as a photographer and is taking photos at Santa's Village."

"Ah. I noticed when I was doing real research she was on the yearbook staff. Guess her love of the camera stuck with her. Also, there were several members of the science club with Mr. Simms. I think we need to talk to him. Teachers have knowledge about cliques and such. We could ask him about Savannah and her mean-girl crew."

True. He'd only been questioned on whether he knew who might have not liked Cora or if she'd ever mentioned boyfriends or wanting to run away—which had been a joke—but that was the only path the detectives at that time had to walk down.

"Miss Poppy!"

Poppy turned and Beth beamed as she stood with her bunny under her arm and a children's book in her hand. Delilah waved.

"Hi, Beth," Poppy said, thankful for the distraction. She didn't want to rehash her high school days or photos with Rhett any further. She returned Delilah's wave.

"I've been to story time," Beth said with pure delight shining in her eyes. Her hair was pulled back in two green barrettes. She was sunshine in a dark place. Everything good about the world.

"You have? What story did you listen to?" Poppy asked.

"*Runaway Bunny.* It's about a bunny that wants to

run away, but his mommy tells him if he runs away she will run after him. We shouldn't run away. We should be who we are."

Poppy grinned, unfamiliar with the storybook. "You're right. You should never run away." If only she'd told Cora that instead of telling her to go. To run to trouble—and ultimately to her death. Instead of telling her to be who she was meant to be, Poppy had persuaded her to be someone else. Someone rebellious disguised as adventurous, out of sheer jealousy and a thirst to have her parents' praise, for once, instead of Cora receiving it. "You're exactly who you're supposed to be, Beth."

Was Poppy? Hadn't she been running since Cora's death—even before?

She couldn't seem to get within two feet of this woman before she wanted to break down. It was as if Beth's purity reflected how filthy Poppy was inside. She wanted to run away. Be someone she wasn't.

"You are too, Poppy," Beth said. "God doesn't make mistakes." She leaned in close. "But people do. I spilled my tea on the carpet this morning. It ran all over and I was scared it would stain the pretty floor, but it didn't. Delilah has special cleaner and I think God uses special cleaner to fix our mistakes." A million-watt smile warmed her face like sunshine. "Have you ever spilled your tea, Poppy?"

She was going to lose it and have a mental breakdown right here in the middle of Gray Creek Library. Her throat grew tight and the backs of her eyes burned like raging fire. She hadn't spilled tea, but she'd made plenty of stains on the carpet of her life and had been trying to scrub them clean ever since. But no matter how much good she did—how many cases she solved and closed—it never removed the stains.

No, she had no special cleaner of her own.

Come now, and let us reason together, saith the Lord: though your sins be as scarlet, they shall be as white as snow; though they be red like crimson, they shall be as wool.

A verse she hadn't thought of in forever struck her heart like a penetrating sword, cutting deep. Was the Lord giving her hope that she could be stain free even after all she'd done? After how far she'd run? How mad she had been at Him? She could remember the insulting words she'd hurled at Him over the years. Could even that be forgiven and cleansed?

"Not tea," she whispered because that was all she had. "But I've made messes. Lots of messes."

"You want to read a book with me?" she asked.

"Oh honey," Delilah interjected, "Agent Holliday has a lot of work to do. She solves cases like Chase in *Paw Patrol*."

"'Chase is on the case!'" Beth cheered. "Do you solve your cases like Chase?"

Poppy had no clue who Chase was, or even what *Paw Patrol* was.

"Agent Poppy," Rhett interjected, "solves more cases than the rest of her team. She's very good and crazy smart."

Poppy's insides slid further into a pile of goo. "I think I have a few minutes to read a story with you." She looked at Rhett and his eyes shone with compassion and something she couldn't quite put her finger on. He gave her a nod and she put her arm around Beth. "What book would you like to read?"

"We can find a Chase-on-the-case book!"

"Sounds perfect."

Poppy spent the next thirty minutes reading books with Beth and talking about how fun it was to live in a B&B and meet new friends each day. Her life was an adventure. Poppy glanced across the library where Rhett sat talking with Delilah. Both had been tasked with the responsibility of caring for their younger sister with some challenges. Poppy had failed. Delilah was thriving with a wonderful business.

Rhett answered his phone and slipped away, then re-entered the library and caught her attention.

Poppy took Beth's hand. "I'm afraid I have to go. Poppy is on the case!"

Beth laughed and walked with her to Delilah and Rhett. He pulled Poppy aside. "I called Mr. Simms. He's out of town and won't return until later tomorrow, but said he'd be happy to talk with us. So I called the former assistant principal—the head principal at that time passed away—and according to her, Savannah, Maya and Natalie terrorized girls who, quote, unquote, got in their way or were rumored to have flirted with or expressed interest in Dylan."

"Like Cora."

"She gave me two names she knew for sure of girls who had been victimized. They had reported them numerous times. Melissa Mann and Candy Banner."

"Who called you? I saw you get up and leave."

"Oh, that was my mom asking about the case and

if it would be wrapped up in time for me to come for Christmas." Torment and sadness darkened his usually warm eyes. She knew that feeling well.

"Maybe you should go. Fly in for Christmas Day. I'll be fine."

"Killer's gonna take Christmas off, you think?"

"If he has any kind of family, I do. And all our suspects have roots here. But who knows. Either way, they clearly miss you."

Her parents had stopped asking if she'd come years ago. They had gone from asking if she would be coming to assuming she wouldn't.

"I know they do. It's just…" His jaw pulsed and he searched her eyes as if wrestling with what he wanted to say next. Finally he blew a heavy breath, and the intensity and turmoil in his eyes disappeared. "And anyway, you'll be alone on Christmas if I leave."

Another wave of mental anguish enveloped her. "I'm alone every Christmas, Rhett. I'm no fun either."

"Well, that's a given," he teased. "I'm not saying I want to spend Christmas with you for any other reason than I know the minute I'm gone you'll do something stupid. Like sneak down chimneys of suspects in a Santa costume to pilfer through their homes for what will surely become inadmissible evidence."

Poppy chuckled. "I could even bug the bows and eat the cookies. I do love cookies."

"And if you do find incriminating evidence, I don't need you hijacking the killer in your Santa sack to take back to the North Pole for torturing—I mean questioning. No, in your case I mean torture." Amusement brought his bereaved eyes back to life.

"You're real proud of your little metaphor, aren't you? And I'd never take him to the North Pole. It's too cold. I hate the cold."

"Which you make known hourly." He rolled his eyes. "It's not a metaphor. It's a—I don't know—a story within a story." He nodded with satisfaction. "And, yes, I am proud."

"Well, speaking of Santa, let's head to his village and talk to Candy Banner. See how naughty Savannah and her minions were."

"Christmas is coming early," Rhett quipped, rubbing his hands together.

Rhett never horsed around like this or humored her ridiculousness. She was seeing a side to him she liked even more—one that was playful and goofy and not so staunch—and therefore it must end, though it was terribly amusing. "Okay, enough with this. It's getting annoying even for me." She paused. "I think it's a play on words."

"Idiom? Which you never get right."

"Hmm…" If he only knew.

They said their goodbyes to Delilah and Beth and rushed out into the frosty air. "I hope this village is in-doors." Poppy shivered. "I really do hate the cold." She bent forward fighting the wind as a brand-new shiver raked over her spine.

"Talk about getting annoying," he muttered.

She ignored him and scanned the charming down-town square. Nothing about this moment was charm-ing. No matter how decorated the boutiques and shops were, or how nice the laughter of people shopping on late lunch breaks was.

Something sinister lurked on the currents of the wintery gales. Invisible eyes on Poppy and Rhett could be felt.

"I got a bad feeling, Wallace," Poppy murmured. "Really bad."

EIGHT

Santa's Village was located inside a small brick activity center with concrete flooring and heat, which was all Poppy cared about. "Holly Jolly Christmas" played in the background as shoppers perused homemade Christmas crafts, candles and goodies. Poppy paused on the boiled peanuts. She hadn't had those since she was a kid. Rhett pointed to the concessions.

"We can make a purchase on our way to talk to Candy Banner."

"Nah. They smell good, though." The crowd was entirely too large for a Monday afternoon. Didn't people work? Her stomach rumbled. "Okay, we do have to eat lunch. And just so you know, if someone is selling turkey legs, it's on."

"Like Donkey Kong." Rhett chuckled as Poppy stepped up to the counter and ordered a warm bag of boiled peanuts. Cajun style. Perfection. She shared a few with him.

"Where's the photos with Santa?"

"Follow the mothers dragging dressed-up, screaming children and we'll be sure to find it." She popped a peanut, shell and all, into her mouth and felt the kick of cayenne. "I need a Coke."

He agreed and bobbed and weaved past the booth stacked with monogrammed stockings. They maneuvered through the large rectangular building until they reached a big sleigh with reindeer and women in elf costumes handing out suckers to children who were in line to tell Santa what they wanted for Christmas. Babies bawled while moms giggled.

Candy stood behind the camera while a young blonde girl shook a jingly toy at a toddler who was having none of it. "You couldn't pay me enough to do this job," Poppy muttered.

"Agreed," Rhett said and snagged a handful of peanuts.

In between kiddos, Poppy approached Candy. The woman was petite. Pretty green eyes. "Candy Banner?"

"Yes."

Poppy made introductions and asked if they could have a moment to speak. "If you give me these next five in line, I'll put a sign out for a break. We could use one." She did appear a little frazzled.

"Sure. We'll look around." Poppy went on the search for a vendor to buy a drink from, and after that they bumped into Delilah and Beth again.

"Are you getting your picture made with Santa?" Beth asked.

"She should," Rhett offered through a chuckle.

"No, we're on a case." Poppy winked at Beth.

"We're going on a train ride next. The Polar Express." Beth beamed and Delilah chuckled.

"It's our annual day to shop and go on the train ride. We wait until Christmas Eve for photos with Santa. The ride is actually pretty fun. They serve cookies and hot chocolate. Only lasts about an hour—a few miles forward then backward. But it's decorated festively and the music gets you in the Christmas spirit."

"You should come!" Beth said. "You get a ticket!"

It was hard to tell this woman no. In so many ways she reminded Poppy of Cora. Kind and trusting and full of wonder and life. The pull to go was strong, but they had so much work to do. People to talk to. Like Candy.

"Well, we'll see." That was the best she could offer. They headed back to Santa's workshop and waited while the last child had his picture made, then Candy yanked off the green elf hat and raked a hand through her hair.

"There's an open food area around back. We can grab a table if that's okay."

They followed her to an area that had been sectioned off with velvet red cording and found a picnic table near the corner. Poppy explained why they were in town.

"I knew Cora," Candy said. "We had algebra together and she helped me out a lot. She was good at math. Me? Not so much."

Poppy sipped her can of Coke. "Did you know Cora had a crush on Dylan Weaverman?"

Candy nodded. "I saw the doodles in the back of her notebook. I warned her that was a bad move."

"Because of Savannah and her entourage of mean girls?" Poppy asked while Rhett sat quietly listening and letting her take the lead.

"They could be spiteful, petty and vindictive." Candy's eyes narrowed.

"We heard you were a target."

Candy groaned. "My freshman year I dropped my backpack and Dylan helped me pick up all the junk and books that had spilled. I thanked him and Savannah saw it all. She spread a vicious rumor about me being pregnant and not knowing who the father was. It was humiliating. She told me if I ever looked at Dylan again, she'd do far worse. She also trashed my car and scratched ugly words into it with her keys—though I couldn't prove it was her or her friends, I know it was."

All for Dylan's kindness. "Did she think you liked him?"

"Anyone who made eye contact with Dylan was obviously in love with him. She did all sorts of mean things to girls over him. And her minions went right along with her. They were her eagle eyes. I don't know what Dylan saw in her. Maybe he was afraid to dump her for fear she'd ruin his life. She had the power to do it."

"And what about now? Are they still mean girls?" Poppy asked.

A kid raced by with a huge corn dog in his hand and his mother chased him down, hollering for him to stop.

"They're still friends but I think they grew out of it. Brad changed Savannah. She was less mean after they started dating. I was shocked when he moved here and she and Dylan were over. I mean, who goes to all that vindictive trouble only to break up a year later?" She sighed. "I'm glad, though. Girls were free from her evil plans."

Maybe it was all water under the bridge then with Maya. But Poppy still wanted to know. "And what about Maya?"

"And my brother? She apologized for her part in my humiliation. I let it go. It could have been worse, I guess. They've only been dating about three months. I don't see it lasting. Maya is a serial dater, if you know what

I mean. I'm more worried about Monty. She's gonna break his heart."

Rhett leaned forward. "Did Savannah know that Cora and Dylan had a crush on each other? What would Savannah do about that back then?"

"If Savannah knew Cora liked Dylan, it would be on, and if it was true that Dylan liked Cora…" Her eyes said it all. Savannah might have done something irreversible. "But the thing is, Savannah usually kept her hands clean and had her girls do the dirty work."

Poppy shared a silent exchange with Rhett.

"Thank you for your time." Poppy stood, and she and Rhett threw away their trash and moved through the hustle and bustle.

"You know, we could take an hour-long train ride," Rhett said. "I can tell you really have a connection with Beth." Mr. Observant hadn't missed that, but it was obvious. And true. "She's really a sweet woman. And I've never been on a train."

"Neither have I." She shrugged.

"We have no leads until we talk to Mr. Simms tomorrow. We could approach Savannah again but she'd likely admit to being mean but not doing anything nefarious to Cora. Let's see what Simms says first. Go from there."

He was right. They had no other leads at the moment and might not have anything more if Simms couldn't give them any insight or new information. They could only hope the lab would find trace evidence on the bomb particles and the debris found in the well. And they still had that bracelet. It could have belonged to any of the girls. Or someone else entirely. Once they had Simms's interview done, she'd go back to the women about their pasts, the bracelet and hopefully new details gained from Simms. She could not fail her family and Cora.

They met up with the Cordray sisters and then followed them to the train station. In line, Delilah leaned over. "It's more crowded at night and the lights are festive, but Beth prefers the daylight trip. I'm glad we can do this. She'd been disappointed when I told her we would be traveling and unable to attend. We rarely travel during the holidays."

"Were you going to visit family?"

"My aunt in Georgia. But she ended up going to California to her brother-in-law's. Our dad passed last year and Mom died three years ago in a car accident."

"I'm sorry."

"Thank you. I've always known Beth would be mine to care for."

Beth was explaining how to paint a rainbow to Rhett, who had given her his undivided attention.

He really was a wonderful man.

She tried not to let the tender moment take root. She refocused on Delilah. "Still, your parents' deaths must have been traumatic for you both."

"It was. Beth was my saving grace. She was grieving, but mostly she wanted to light up my life and comfort me. She is a comfort." She grinned as Beth prattled on with Rhett.

"Was it hard for you? Growing up with Beth?"

Delilah's laugh was wistful. "At times. I felt neglected. She took up a lot of Mom and Dad's attention. But it was hard to be angry at her."

Poppy had been mad at Cora so many times. Jealous of her.

"But there were times I was bitterly jealous. Now, she's all I have and I love her dearly. She's a joy to all our guests too. She's special and precious." Delilah wiped a tear. "I worry about what will happen if something happens to me. I pray God keeps me going so I can tend to her."

"She is special. I've enjoyed being around her." That was about all Poppy could say. What would happen to Beth if her sister tragically died? The thought concerned her. It would be too easy for her to be taken advantage of.

They received their tickets and entered a train car. White lights and pine garland draped the windows. Little Christmas trees were anchored to each table, and Santa's helpers came through delivering sugar cookies and hot chocolate in red and green insulated cups. The soundtrack from *The Polar Express* played in the background, and the engineer came through and greeted everyone. He was dressed like the engineer from the movie.

The whistle blew then they were off down the tracks. They sang Christmas carols and enjoyed the wooded scenery on either side of the train. Snow flurries swirled against the dusky sky then dusted the trees and grass. Kids clapped and stuck their noses against the windows. Some of them had probably never witnessed real snow.

Cora would have loved a Christmas train ride.

"I'm going to find a restroom," Poppy said and exited the car, moving into the next one. A helper told her there was a bathroom at the end of the carriage. She thanked her and maneuvered to the car next to the caboose.

She paused before entering the ladies' room. The hairs on her neck prickled, but the car was empty. She entered and splashed water on her face. She hadn't wanted to ruin anyone's enjoyment but Cora weighed heavily on her mind and she had needed a moment. Once she toweled off her face, she exited the ladies' room.

That same creepy feeling came over her again. She started back toward her car but a man burst out from under one of the tables, charging her and shoving her to the floor as she reached for her gun. He caught what she was doing, and they struggled for the weapon; he batted her hand against the floor and she lost it.

Poppy screamed, hoping someone might hear her, but the odds were slim with the loud music and even louder children. They were several empty cars away from people. But she tried anyway and fought and clawed. If she could tear away his ski mask…identify him…

His gloved hands wrapped around her throat and squeezed. The pressure was unbearable, burning. Fighting to free her leg, she kneed him, then scrambled up but there was nowhere to go. He blocked her path to freedom. Her gun was across the floor behind him. The only way out of this alive was to fight her way out.

She braced herself as he shoved her against the train car door. She punched him in the side, connected with ribs and heard him grunt. He wasn't getting out of this unscathed no matter how it went down for her. Poppy would leave a distinguishing mark and Rhett would observe it. It was his superpower. Her attacker's body pressed against hers, pinning her legs, and she headbutted him—her own brain seeming to rattle around from the force.

He growled and released the door handle, shoving it open.

Frigid wind knocked her off balance and she grabbed the handicap rails and braced her feet against each side of the threshold to keep from tumbling out. The roar of the engine was deafening.

In a battle of tangled limbs, Poppy fought to stay inside as the assailant used all his force to shove her out.

The door to the car opened, drawing their attention, and Poppy froze. No! Beth entered with her little bunny. Poppy's lungs turned to iron.

"Hi, Poppy."

The attacker paused as if unsure what to do. Poppy couldn't push past him, couldn't do anything without Beth becoming collateral damage.

Poppy had no other options. Beth would not lose her life by being in the wrong place at the wrong time.

Poppy grabbed the attacker's coat collar, then let her foot go, startling him as she took him off the side of the train with her.

Rhett finished off his hot chocolate as Delilah discussed her plans for opening another B&B with a friend in the next county. Suddenly Beth rushed into the car, tears streaming down her cheeks.

"Honey, what's wrong?" Delilah asked. "Could you not find the bathroom?"

"Poppy jumped off the train."

Rhett went on high alert. "What?"

"She jumped off the train with a man in a mask."

Rhett bolted, his blood racing wildly as he raced to the bathrooms. How had a killer gotten on the train? How would he have even known he'd have a chance to attack Poppy? So many questions peppered his mind. At the back car, the door was open.

The train wasn't moving incredibly fast, but enough to cause broken bones or other injuries. Had he shoved her off the train? Beth said she jumped. If she jumped off after the killer...

Rhett scanned the woods for any sign of her or the masked attacker, his heart hammering against his ribs.

Poppy was out there with a murderer. Possibly injured and vulnerable. He was wasting time standing here. Without weighing consequences or the danger, he leaped out of the train, landing on the hard, cold ground and jarring his teeth. His head thudded on impact, and his hip took the brunt. He rolled several times and ended up on his back, the breath knocked from his lungs.

Forcing himself to stand on wobbly legs, he pushed forward and in the direction she might have fallen.

Panic and terror pumped his feet faster. He surveyed the woods, hoping to catch a glimpse of her, when a gunshot rang out and his blood curdled.

"Poppy!" he bellowed and pushed even harder, faster.

In the distance, he spotted her darting into the tree line. Rhett fired into the woods, opposite Poppy as not to hit her, but hoping to scare the attacker from shooting again.

Praise the Lord. She was upright and alive.

"Poppy!" he hollered again. No more shots were fired. The attacker was likely jetting through the woods. Rhett found her a few feet inside the thick covering of trees, bent over at the waist panting. Red marks colored her neck; dirt and scratches covered her cheeks. Her pants and sweater were torn. Rhett closed the distance between them and took her by the shoulders, unsure if he wanted to kiss her or shake her for scaring him half to death—or both.

"Did you—did you jump off a train for me?" she asked.

Heat climbed up his neck. "I guess I did." Without any real thought too. No calculating risks. Just taking a dangerous one. He was going to have to chew on the reason why he would do something that cowboy-like. "Are you hurt?"

"I'm gonna have severe bruises. He came out of nowhere. He must have gotten on the train and tucked himself into an empty car hoping for a chance to get me alone, but that was a long shot."

"It's a desperate move on his part. We're getting close somehow—maybe by following the drugs. There was no guarantee he'd get you or me alone. Unless he was already on the ride and used it as an opportunity."

"And he happens to keep a ski mask in his pocket?" She raked a hand through her tangled hair. "Who carries those?"

"Anyone. Hunters? He shot off through the woods like a man who knew them well." Rhett brushed some dirt from her cheek. Another impulsive move. They were becoming one too many. "Did you jump off to catch him?"

Poppy caressed her cheek as if she could still feel his touch. "No." She told him about Beth interrupting and how her only choice was to jump and take him with her. Now he didn't want to shake her. Just kiss her. She was selfless. Brave. Willing to sacrifice herself. She laughed. "He may have been my saving grace. I landed on him and he took the brunt of the fall."

Rhett balled his hands at his side to keep from drawing her into his arms. No more impulsive decisions today. "Once you landed, what happened?"

"I bounced off him and rolled, knocking my breath from me. I sat up and he was still catching his breath. I took off running and he shot at me. Then you fired and sent him farther into the woods. He got away. Again," she said with force. "But he's got to be wounded too. Bruised. Battered. Scratches. Something. That may be to our benefit."

Definitely. "Do you need a doctor?"

"No. But I'm gonna need a bottle of aspirin and a few ice packs." She rubbed her lower back. "You?"

"I'm feeling it. You know, I used to leap off the couch, pretending it was a train and I was catching robbers. Never really thought I'd actually do it in real life. Doesn't quite feel like jumping onto a pile of pillows."

Poppy snickered. "Sure, it does. If the pillows are made of concrete." She surveyed the area. "Now we get to work out the sore muscles by hoofing it back to town. You think when the train comes back through it'll stop for us?"

They followed the tracks that led back to the station. "Doubtful." After a few moments of silence Rhett spoke up. "That was a brave thing you did to protect Beth. I'm proud of you. Don't get me wrong—you scared me half to death. Beth came back crying saying you'd jumped off the train with a man in a mask and... Well, I'm proud of you, Doc." He winked and she laughed.

"I'm no daisy."

Rhett chuckled and it hurt his sides as she referred back to their favorite Western film. Wyatt Earp. Doc Holliday. No, she was not a wimp. She was tough and brave—which he admired, but what had driven her to jump off a train to protect Beth wasn't her tough side; it was the deeply tender and caring side that she often tried to hide. The side he had seen more of in the past few days than in the few years of their working relationship. And he wasn't sure what to do with that.

His physical attraction toward her was no big deal. Plenty of women were attractive, but it wasn't simply physical, and that presented a problem.

Because he feared his dive off that moving train was motivated by far more than backing up his colleague.

The train passed them, moving slowly enough for him to catch a glimpse of a worried Delilah looking out the window. "You have Delilah's number?"

"No. Just the number to the B&B. Do you think she tried to get the engineer to stop?"

Rhett shrugged as the caboose passed them by. "Too bad we can't jump back on like we jumped off."

She snort-laughed and grabbed her side. "I don't think I can hop a puddle let alone a train, Wallace. Slow and stealthy is about all I got in me."

It had only been a matter of time before she messed up an idiom again. But he found he wasn't as annoyed as before… It was…no. He was not going to think of it as endearing. "Steady. It's slow and steady."

"Whatever, Wallace," she quipped with her usual amount of indifference and snarl. But that ship had sailed. Her gruffness and sharp teeth were nothing more than a façade covering up the real Poppy Holliday—the woman who was willing to sacrifice herself for the people she cared about, and there was no mistaking that Poppy had grown to care for Beth in the short amount of time she'd known her. There was no bite along with that bark. It was nothing more than a defense mechanism.

But why use defenses against him?

"I'm just saying."

Finally, they made it to the train station, where they found Delilah and Beth frantically talking to the manager. Beth spotted Poppy and squealed, and Delilah visibly relaxed. They came running and Beth wrapped her arms around Poppy. "I prayed for you, Poppy."

"Thank you, hon. I needed it."

Delilah hugged them too. "We told the train employees what happened, but they wouldn't stop even when they found the door open. I was terrified and trying to get them to go back out there and look for you. What on earth happened?"

Poppy glanced at Beth. "Beth, you want to go get a Coke?" She and Beth left Rhett with Delilah so he could explain without terrifying her sister or causing her anxiety.

"I need to call the sheriff."

"Rudy would want to know for sure."

Rhett raised his eyebrows. He'd noticed Delilah was on a first-name basis with him the night of the explosion, and he was familiar with Beth too. "You two close?"

Delilah's cheeks flushed. "It's complicated. His wife left him and took their daughter. We…had some things in common, but we both knew if there was a chance to reconcile, he needed to take it, and there might be. We're friends."

Then why the interest in Poppy? Because it was hard not to be attracted to her, or maybe Rhett had misinterpreted his appreciation and kind gestures because… because he'd been jealous.

How ridiculous could Rhett be?

Poppy and Beth returned with drinks. She gave Rhett a bottle of water. Hers was over half-empty already.

After leaving the train station, Poppy had called the sheriff to let him know what had transpired and that they were coming into the SO now to give statements.

"After statements, I want a soft bed and several hours of sleep."

"Best idea all day," she said. "Tomorrow we'll start fresh with Solomon Simms."

Surely, they'd get a few hours of uninterrupted sleep. But the way their days were going, that might not be possible. Not when a killer had been thrust from a train and had almost been taken out by the one woman he was targeting. He'd be furious and even more determined.

And that meant Rhett wouldn't be sleeping.

Not when his number-one priority was keeping Poppy safe.

NINE

Poppy woke up the next morning aching and sore. A hot shower had helped with the tight muscles, and pain medication had taken off the edge, but her head still ached and she was in a crummy mood.

Rhett hadn't been a peach to be around either. They'd tested each other's nerves over breakfast and he'd answered most of her questions in grunts as they drove to the sheriff's office, but he'd used actual words with Sheriff Pritchard, Detective Teague and Detective Banner during an update and briefing about the attacks and the news that Dylan's death was being ruled an accident due to drunk driving.

Poppy noted they should push harder, and that maybe Detective Teague wasn't doing his best since his wife could be involved.

That had gone over about as well as feeding steak to a toothless baby. Teague had choked on it and spit it out. Maybe Poppy had been harsh and overly critical due to the pain and the fact that they were no further in the case than she'd been before. All she had to show for her investigative efforts were dozens of bruises, aches and pains.

Sheriff Pritchard had reminded her she wasn't here to investigate Dylan's death or play judge over teenagers' past behavior.

But if Savannah's behavior was directly linked to Cora's murder, then it had to be followed. If Dylan had hurt Cora, or if Savannah had—with intent or accidentally—Teague wasn't the one Poppy wanted on the case. But neither was Monty Banner. Because Savannah wasn't the only mean girl. Poppy had to look at Maya Marx and Natalie Carpenter-Weaverman and Ian Kirkwood. Any one of them, or all of them, could have harmed Cora.

And there was still Dylan Weaverman himself. He could have been overcome with guilt and taken his life for a part he'd played in Cora's death. Or he could have been killed because he wanted to go to the authorities about Cora when her body was found. The timeline was too close, and she wasn't buying that his death was an accident—though he had been drinking enough to be drunk. Anyone who knew him knew he had an alcohol problem, which meant someone could have used that to his or her advantage.

Somehow.

She pinched the bridge of her nose and paced the small room they'd been using as a work space. They'd come in around ten and it was nearing noon now. Simms would be back in town soon. She was champing at the bit to talk to him.

If Solomon Simms had heard plans to harm or even humiliate Cora and done nothing about it, he'd rue the day he sat on his hands.

She couldn't wait around and do nothing, and Dylan's death was still gnawing at her.

She grabbed her phone off the table and called his older brother, Zack. He answered on the third ring. "Agent Holliday. How are you today?"

News had spread fast about what she and Rhett had gone through yesterday, and of course their cars blowing up had been the talk of the town. "I'm alive and that's about all I can say so far. I wanted to talk to you about your brother again."

"Sure." A door clicked and the background grew quiet. "I'm helping out my wife today and the animals don't know how to stay silent during a phone call."

Poppy waited for him to get settled.

"Sheriff Pritchard told me they ruled Dylan's death accidental. Is there something new in the case?"

"I'm struggling with the fact his accident happened the same night that the remains of my sister were found on your property. And what was he doing out that time of night?"

"He was drinking, Agent. I doubt we'll know the answer to that."

"What if he was going out to the property? Looking for something? Or what if he was there because he felt bad about something that happened in the past?"

"You think my little brother killed your sister and was out there drunk, looking for incriminating evidence? He'd have fallen down that well too."

"I never said anything about looking for evidence down a well."

"Wouldn't that be the obvious place?"

Poppy's gut roiled. "Do you know anything about that night, Zack? Maybe he got drunk. Did something he'd never have done sober. Maybe he told you. We found a bracelet in that well. Know anyone who might have worn a silver bracelet? Let me send you a photo." She put him on speaker and sent the photo of the evidence.

"I don't know anything. My brother didn't do any…" He trailed off as the text came through and the line went silent for a few beats. "I don't recognize that bracelet."

"Maybe Dylan would. Maybe he knew it would be found and decided to come forward. Maybe the owner of that bracelet silenced him before he could and planned to take her chances of it never being linked to her." It could have belonged to any of the mean girls. And Natalie Carpenter-Weaverman had a lot to lose. A husband, a vet practice…her freedom. She and the whole gang she kept close tabs on would lose a lot. No one got a chance to snag that piece of jewelry—if that was what the killer was out there doing that night. Ian Kirkwood. Zack Weaverman himself. Or someone else who had been involved that night they didn't know about.

"Or maybe it fell down there another time. At another party. Prior to your sister's death."

"Maybe. But someone is going to recognize it. Show it to Natalie. See if she does. She was tight with Dylan then and leading up to his death. She went to those parties. She knew Cora. That's all I'm saying."

"The next time you have something to say, you can do it with our lawyers present." He hung up. Rhett entered the room. His eyes looked tired, with dark half moons underneath. A sudden urge to hug and soothe him overcame her, and before she could talk herself out of it, she was on her feet and twining her arms around his back with her head tucked under his chin. His muscles tensed against hers as if he'd been expecting a foe rather than a friend, but then he relaxed and his hands rested lightly on her upper back.

"I'm sorry for all that's happened, Rhett. I didn't want any of this for you." Most of the night she'd been awake picturing him leaping off the train to rescue her and poking at the idea that there had been more to the risk than saving a colleague in danger, but she didn't attempt to explore the idea further out of sheer terror.

Yet here she was hugging him, feeling that same sense of safety and the security of hope and home fill her. "I mean, I told you I'd take every measure to find who killed Cora. I never expected you to."

"You were in trouble. What other option did I have?"

He could have pulled rank and had the train stopped. Or called the sheriff. Or both.

Jumping off the train was reckless. Impulsive. It went against the grain of who Rhett was.

"You had options," she murmured.

Rhett's chin rested on her head. "The only option was getting to you."

Like the mom in *Runaway Bunny.* Pursuing the little bunny because he belonged to her. Chasing him down. Being exactly what he needed in every situation.

A verse that her mother always spoke over them before bedtime swept across her heart.

Fear not, for I have redeemed thee; I have called thee by thy name; thou art Mine.

Thou art Mine. Pursued. Loved. Redeemed. A statement of belonging. A statement that should bring peace to a fearful, searching heart. In Rhett's arms, at least right now, she felt like she might belong.

One thing was for sure: she felt no fear in this moment.

Confess your faults one to another, and pray one
for another, that ye may be healed.

She hadn't thought of these Scriptures in years, and
they rushed into her memory now like a warm flood, as
if they'd never left her heart. Would confession do her
heart good? Bring healing? Poppy was like a sweater
being eaten by moths. Gaping holes destroying what
was once lovely and useful.

Withdrawing from Rhett, she gazed into his eyes.
"It's my fault Cora is dead. I've never told anyone that.
I was jealous of her sickness—it's horrible, I know. I
wished I could be ill because then I'd have my parents' attention and unconditional love. I wouldn't have
to be responsible for someone else. Others would tend
to and take care of me. What kind of person is jealous
over their sister's suffering? Delilah finds it a joy to
care for Beth."

Rhett already thought she was a piece of work. How
much more judgment could he unleash?

Tears filled her eyes and held, refusing to fall. "I was
livid that she was everything good and I had to act like
a fool to gain one scrap of attention. And that's what I
did, Rhett. I acted foolishly and it never worked. But I
kept doing it and expecting the same result—love from
my parents. That's the very definition of insanity."

A hot tear slipped out of her eye, and Rhett caught it
with his fingertip while his fingers remained cradling
her cheek. "You were a girl with a girl's mind. You
loved your sister. I know you did. Love is complicated."

Love was complicated. "I did—I do love her. But..."
She touched his fingers, and her stomach fluttered. "I've
never been in love...while I'm confessing."

He held her gaze and swallowed, his Adam's apple bobbing. "Neither have I."

But a truth whispered to her heart and she shut it out before it formed into words and could take root. She hadn't meant to go down this road, but her tongue had a mind of its own. She reeled back to where the topic of confession was supposed to be. On Cora. Not Poppy's heart. "I told Cora she never allowed herself to live and be free. That at least I was living my life and would have no regrets." She shook her head. "But I have so many of them. My accusations and that argument caused Cora to take chances she normally wouldn't. She looked up to me. Loved me. I drove her to hold that pot for a friend. And it was my words that fueled her to sneak out of the house that night. To go live a life of no regrets."

Torment flashed in Rhett's eyes and he pursed his lips. "Poppy, you are not to blame for her death."

"Except that I am. And now you know why I have to knock down every door and walk into every situation to bring her justice. But I don't expect you to do that too. You can't be jumping trains, Rhett. Not for me. I can't have any more deaths on my hands. I have enough blood there already."

If anyone could relate to Poppy's guilt, it was Rhett. But his situation had been much different. Poppy couldn't be blamed for choices Cora made over an argument, but Rhett had known the ice was dangerous— that's why it had been a dare. His action forced Keith's hand. If he'd have only turned down the dare.

But he hadn't.

And Poppy was right. He'd had other options concerning her safety after she jumped off the train, but he'd done what would get to her fastest—he'd leaped. Looking into her eyes in this moment, he wanted to take another leap.

But he wouldn't.

"Let me worry about my decisions. They are mine alone. We're a team. We have each other's backs. That's the job." He could keep telling himself that, but underneath the surface he knew it had become something more, something he continued to fight tooth and nail. He wasn't sure if he had enough strength to keep it up, but he'd have to muster it from deep down. He wanted predictable. Safe. Structured. Didn't want to get involved with someone he worked with for fear they wouldn't last, and then there would be too many complications.

Love was complicated. No…he wasn't going to admit to that emotion. He'd lose the battle if he let that word linger in his brain and on his tongue. Hearing her confession hadn't helped in the fight; it had only served to connect him even more deeply. He'd harbored the same thoughts and feelings, but Poppy had bared it all—to him alone. Her choice to share it with him revealed her level of trust and vulnerability.

He didn't owe her his own confession. Shouldn't reveal it for fear of what his own vulnerability might do, but he leaped anyway out of a compelling need for her to know how much he did understand her, how much he could identify.

"Poppy, I understand you more than you realize. I have a confession of my own that I've never told anyone either. You know my brother died. And that he drowned. But I get how you feel, because Keith's death actually was my fault." Saying those words out loud released some pent-up agony, especially when he saw compassion and not criticism in Poppy's eyes. No one could understand his sorrow like she did. He preceded to finish the sordid tale.

"That's why I don't go home at Christmas. When the ice cracked, my insides did too. I should've plunged in after him. I didn't. I stood in shock while he drowned. You'd think it'd be loud, you know? But it's deathly silent. After the initial struggle…it goes so quiet."

Poppy wiped her eyes and squeezed him until he felt completely safe, completely accepted even after sharing his darkest shame. He clung to her and buried his face in her hair, enjoying this freedom of being fully known yet still welcomed into an embrace.

"You make so much more sense now, Rhett. Why you calculate everything. Are overly cautious."

Exactly. The very reasons he couldn't be with her, and yet here he was hanging on to her like a lifeline. "This is why I know you're not to blame for Cora's death. You got in a typical sibling argument. Cora made her choice."

She pulled away and poked a finger in his chest. "And you were a boy taking a boy's dare. You panicked and the current took him under the ice, but if you had jumped in you'd have died."

And yet he'd jumped for her.

The door opened, jarring the moment, jarring his thoughts. Poppy stepped away and Detective Banner raised his eyebrows. That was twice he'd found them in what could appear an intimate moment. In its own way, it was the most intimate moment he'd ever shared with anyone—and he'd shared it with her.

Now what was he supposed to do?

"Solomon Simms is here. Said you had called and wanted to talk him. Got in to town a few minutes early and was in the neighborhood. He's in interview room one." He paused and batted a glance between them. "Y'all need another minute?"

"No," Poppy said. She had already snatched up her legal pad and pen and was striding to the door.

Rhett followed her into the interview room, where a man who looked more like a coach than a science teacher sat with a small cup of coffee. He was dressed in jeans and a button-down shirt with a gray cardigan over it. His buzzed hair was silvery blond.

"Mr. Simms," Poppy said. "Thank you for coming in of your own accord. I appreciate that."

Because he'd come in on his own, or because it cut short what had been happening between them?

"I want to help. I liked Cora. She was bright and an all-around sweet girl." Mr. Simms leaned forward, his arms on the table.

Poppy sat across from him. "I never had the privilege of taking one of your classes."

How old was this guy? He couldn't be but maybe a decade or so older than Poppy, putting him in his late twenties or early thirties back when they were in high school. No wonder the kids loved him. He wouldn't have been much more than one himself then.

"What can you tell us about the science club members, specifically Natalie Carpenter, Dylan Weaverman, Ian Kirkwood, Maya Marx and Savannah Steadman?"

"You think one of them had something to do with Cora's death?" Skepticism drew a line across his brow.

"Maybe."

Simms said he didn't believe any of them were capable of murder, and he wasn't aware of drugs being sold. However, he'd been fairly certain that Dylan liked Cora. "He tried to be her lab partner before Natalie could claim him as her own. I think she had an ulterior motive."

"Keeping Cora and Dylan apart?"

Mr. Simms leaned back in his chair. "Yes, but I don't think it was at Savannah's request. I suspected Natalie had a secret crush on Dylan herself."

This changed the game altogether. "After Savannah and Dylan broke up the following year, who did Natalie date? Surely you have an idea."

"I wouldn't say they dated, but Dylan and Natalie became inseparable. Even through college and up until she married Zack." Simms rubbed his chin and smirked. "I guess she ended up with the second-best brother."

Poppy held out her phone. "You recognize this bracelet?"

He studied the photo. "I can't say that I do. Sorry."

Poppy leaned forward. "Do you think Dylan would have hurt Cora?"

"No way. Dylan was a great kid. I'm not real sure what he was doing with Savannah Steadman. The best thing that happened to him, in my opinion, was Savannah meeting Brad Teague. I think things changed—she changed."

"Do you think if something went down with Cora involving Savannah and her cronies, he would have known?"

Dylan's death could have easily been over Cora. They needed some solid evidence. Rhett studied Mr. Simms's wheels turning. "I don't think so. But I don't really know."

They saw him out and Poppy rubbed her temples. "We may have been going at this all wrong. If Natalie had a secret crush on Dylan and knew he liked Cora she may have had as much reason to get rid of her as Savannah had. She could have done something to my sister with the false pretense she was helping Savannah. All the while setting her own sights on him." She huffed. "Dylan is the key to this thing. My gut says so. Those girls and Ian Kirkwood are hiding the truth."

"What if Natalie was never over Dylan? What if they had a thing and his drinking was guilt over an affair all these years later, and not Cora's death? What if Zack found out and used the opportunity to kill him?"

"And the web thickens."

Rhett chuckled. "No. The *plot thickens.* The web is tangled. 'Oh, what a tangled web we weave.'"

"Either way," she said and lifted a shoulder. "We need to go back to all of them with this new information."

"I understand, but her husband needs some courtesy. She's more of a suspect now."

"That's fair."

Detective Teague's pen hung from his teeth as he clacked away on his computer. A mound of files sat beside him, along with a cup of coffee. He glanced up and spoke without removing the pen from between his teeth. "Agents."

"Detective," Poppy said, keeping her voice soft and friendly. "We need to inform you that our investigation is leading to your wife, as well as her friends, due to some ill-behaved-girl stuff involving Cora. We're going to have to pursue that lead."

He removed the pen from his lips and frowned. "You

think Savannah may have knowledge of what happened to your sister?"

Knowledge...bloody hands...

"I don't know. Not until we talk to her again, but we felt you should know. I'm not sure if you're aware of Savannah's reputation in high school—"

"That she could be cruel to other girls?" His face softened. "Yeah. I know. She came from a home that looked happy on the outside, but inside was a rotten mess. Kind of like her as a teenager. She regrets the things she did back then and has even made amends to some of the girls she hurt. But she wouldn't physically hurt anyone, let alone murder them."

Poppy nodded as if she was in complete agreement with the detective. "I'm sorry about her childhood. Hurt people...hurt people. I know that well. But we do need to talk to her again, along with her closest girlfriends at that time, and it won't be as gentle, I'm afraid. Someone in that circle of friends—maybe all of them—is lying."

He paused and worked his jaw, but then he nodded. "I appreciate the heads-up."

Detective Banner breezed inside with a plastic bag that smelled amazing. Rhett was starving. He set it on Teague's desk. "What's going on here?"

Teague sighed. "Their investigation is leading them to Savannah—and Maya."

Monty Banner paused, then picked up his carton of chicken and dumplings and stabbed one with his fork. "Is that why you were at the clinic the other day? You think Maya was involved with your sister's death?"

"I don't know. But that's the only trail we have right now. So we're gonna hunt and sniff out what we can."

She nodded toward the food. "Where'd you get that? It looks amazing."

"It is," Monty said with a grin "Little Evergreen Café. Over by the Christmas Tree Farm. On Hull Road."

After a few more minutes of chitchat, they left the sheriff's office for lunch at the café.

Inside the tiny but cozy establishment decorated with all sizes of artificial pine trees, rustic tin, burlap and red trucks, Rhett guided her to a small table by the window, giving them a gorgeous view of the tree farm across the road. They scanned the brown paper menus in silence, then placed their orders for chicken and dumplings, green beans and corn muffins, along with sweet tea.

Poppy seemed deep in thought, staring off at the trees. "We never had a real Christmas tree," she said as the server brought their big glasses of honey-brown tea. One sip proved it was as sweet as it was big.

"We did. I personally haven't put up a tree in years. My sister bought me one of those little trees with fiber-optic lights. It sits on my breakfast bar. That's about as decorative as I get. Christmas doesn't have the same excitement since Keith died." There wasn't much festivity left.

"You know," she said, "we might not be big on Christmas anymore but you know who is? Delilah and Beth. And you know what we ruined? Their Christmas tree. She said she was going to buy a pre-lit artificial when she had a chance now that the porch and windows are fixed, but we could always go next door and cut down some Christmas cheer. Besides, I could use some cheer right now. I'm feeling extremely noncheery."

He tossed the wadded-up straw paper at her nose.

"Poppy, sometimes you have great ideas. Not always. But sometimes."

It had been ages since he'd gone out in the cold, smelled the pine and picked out a Christmas tree. He and Keith had always agreed on the same one.

Poppy ignored his teasing and drank her tea until their food arrived and they dug into their delicious lunch, barely speaking while they devoured it. After paying, they left the warm atmosphere of the hometown café for the gusty wind and pewter skies.

At the Christmas Tree Farm, they were told they could have their pick delivered. Which was a good thing since they didn't have a truck. Neither of them even owned a car right now.

The gales picked up and icy wind raced down the neck of his sweater but he didn't mind; his blood had been racing hot for days. The farm was void of customers and they had the pick of the litter.

"I like that one," Rhett said, pointing toward a medium-sized one. "Not too full. Not Charlie Brown pitiful either."

"Yeah. That's a pretty one." She nodded in satisfaction. "Tonight might actually be fun. I could use some—"

A shot rang out and the tree branches near Poppy's head exploded.

TEN

Rhett grabbed Poppy around her waist and tossed her to the ground, shielding her with his body. "I don't know how far away the shots are coming from," he said through a strained whisper.

"I don't want to stick around to find out." Adrenaline jolted her system, sending her pulse spiking to dangerous levels.

"Me neither." Rhett drew his weapon and Poppy followed suit, hunching and keeping close to the branches for cover as they sprinted down the rows of trees.

Another projectile was fired and Poppy felt the sting and burn. "I've been grazed!" She grabbed her shoulder. Rhett halted but she motioned him to keep moving. "I'm fine. Let's change direction." Attempting to sound in control proved difficult. Fear propelled her forward as they pushed between the trees instead of running down the smooth paths between them.

Blindly running, they had no clue what was on the other side of the tree farm. Likely more woods, and the shooter had an advantage—he was probably local. Poppy hadn't lived here long enough to know all the trails, woods and back roads.

"Where are we going?" she asked as Rhett led the charge, as if he knew exactly where they were headed.

"Away."

If the situation wasn't life-threatening, she'd have laughed. Away. Good call.

Another shot sounded and instinctively she ducked. The shooter was close enough to get the shots off but far enough back they couldn't see him. Zigging and zagging, they maneuvered out of the trees and to a back road.

They could run down the pavement and hope for a car or take their chances in the woods. Neither option was great. "I don't know what to do!" Poppy declared.

"Woods. We're open targets and he's using a rifle. No way he can see us without a scope. We have a better chance of finding a hiding spot." Rhett motioned to keep running. Poppy pulled out her phone and saw she had a signal. She called 911.

"911. What's your emergency?"

"This is MBI Agent Poppy Holliday. My partner and I are being pursued by a gunman north of the Evergreen. Dispatch units immediately. We are in the woods behind the farm. About a quarter of a mile in." She hung up and pocketed her phone as she leaped over a large dead tree trunk that had fallen.

"Maybe sirens will call him off."

Another shot was fired.

"Up ahead. See that dead hollow tree? We're going in it."

"But he might see us!"

"The bullet would have made a closer connection if he could see us. For now, he's flying blind too. But not for long." Rhett tugged her to the huge fallen tree and she crawled inside the earthy, mushy trunk. The smell of dead animals and rotten leaves thumped her gag reflex. Rhett wiggled in next to her and they lay on their sides, literally nose to nose.

"Be still," he whispered and she caught the hint of mint on his breath, felt his chest rising and falling against hers. Their hands touched. She didn't bother attempting to shift away—there was nowhere to go, and there was nothing romantic about this situation.

Leaves and twigs crunched and snapped, the sounds coming closer. Poppy held her breath. If the killer had any inkling of their location, they might as well be in a coffin as their death was guaranteed.

Another wave of panic washed over her, inducing uncontrollable shudders. Rhett intertwined his fingers with hers, the warmth steadying her. "It's okay," he soothed through a whisper as his forehead pressed into hers, another reassuring and comforting gesture.

Was it okay? No. Nothing was certain. Rhett had to be going bonkers. He thrived on structure, plans and routine. If ever life was chaotic and out of control, it was now. Being stuffed in a tree trunk was a far cry from his carefully crafted life—all due to one teenage slipup. She didn't fault him for Keith's death. But his circumstances were nothing like Poppy's.

A thud on the tree trunk sent Poppy's blood whooshing in her ears.

The killer was standing on them! Did he know it? Was this his cruel way of clueing them in on the fact they were cornered? Poppy squeezed Rhett's hand tighter.

Heavy boots scraped across the tree trunk, and small specks of wood shook loose from above, dusting their heads. Poppy's nose burned and tickled. No. Now was not the time to sneeze. She wiggled her nose, working the sneeze away.

If she could finagle her gun into her hand, she could start shooting; this definitely qualified as a life-threatening situation, but Poppy wanted Cora's killer to rot in a cell, and a dead man couldn't give up anyone else's part in Cora's death. She didn't believe whoever was after her now had acted alone then.

One was already dead and unable to talk.

The trunk shook and footfalls crunched along the ground again, growing fainter with each step until silence loomed.

Rhett's body relaxed against hers. "I think we're in the clear."

The gunman must have used the trunk to gain a better view. "I'm scared to find out."

"Do you wanna lay inside this dead tree all day?" he murmured.

"Kinda…no."

They'd released pent-up breaths, but not their intertwined fingers, and neither was making any effort to let go. But a killer was on the loose and Poppy couldn't hang out in a tree k-i-s-s-i-n-g all day. She broke the hold.

"I'll go first. Cover me." Rhett shimmied his way out of the trunk and Poppy moved quickly to gain a clear view and watch his back. They stood listening and watching. Waiting.

When it felt secure, they trudged back toward the Christmas Tree Farm. "How did he know where we were? We're not even using the same cars."

"No. No, he blew those up." Rhett sighed. "Ian Kirkwood is military. He'd have the skills to follow, scope us and hunt us—not to mention he loves hunting in general.

He knows this town, these woods. But we can't prove anything. I wish there was a way to get him to confess."

"He doesn't know we don't have proof. We could work that in our favor." Fudging the truth wasn't off the table. Police did it often. Rhett wasn't a fan, though.

He didn't reply. Maybe he was becoming as desperate as Poppy.

"I don't know," he finally said. "This is going to sound crazy given our situation presently and especially coming from me, but I think we should still buy a tree for the Cordrays. I know we should head straight to Ian Kirkwood's and we still have to talk to Savannah—but I'll be honest... I need a minute after all that. I'm sorry. I know this is about Cora—"

"Okay." Poppy understood and agreed. Almost every day—and sometimes twice a day—they'd been targets and their bodies were shot. Literally. It was fogging their minds. One night off wouldn't kill them—she hoped.

Poppy's phone buzzed in her pocket. Her brother. "Hey, Tack."

"Hey," he said in his baritone voice. "Wanted to see where you were on the case and let you know that I'm taking off for a while. My case will be there when I get back. You gonna come home for Christmas?"

"No. I can't. Besides, they don't really want me there anyway."

"Not true."

Tack was the golden boy. He had no idea what it felt like to be the black sheep.

"We're making some headway."

"Yeah?"

She explained her theory and reluctantly told him about the attacks, the second blown-up car and the graze on her arm, which burned like crazy. "But we're handling it."

Radio silence hung in the air before Tack sighed heavily, clearly unhappy with the turn of events and the fact that his little sister had become a target. "I can be there by nightfall."

"No." She had made the mess and would clean it up by bringing justice and closure. "Rhett and I are being careful."

Rhett's eyebrow twitched north and she grinned. Caution hadn't actually kept them from danger. Sounded good, though. "We're watching our backs." As the killer shot at them. "Go home for the holidays, Tack. If I need you, I'll call you."

"Bunk. But okay."

"I'm serious. See you soon." She hung up. "He's overprotective and competitive. He probably wants to prove he can solve this case before I can."

"Or he wants one sister safe, and justice for his other sister." Rhett hopped a log.

"Do you always have to be so reasonable?" she griped.

"Do you always have to jump to the worst conclusion?" he countered.

"Whatever," she muttered as the tree farm came into view. "Bah humbug."

Tousling her hair, he chuckled. "This was originally your idea."

"I know. And you said it was a good one." She tromped toward the front of the farm to give an employee the number of the tree they'd chosen.

"Doubtful you'll hear that again." He waved over an attendant. "Ready to make a family happy?"

ELEVEN

Tuesday slipped into Wednesday and then into Thursday. Rhett's mom had called one last time, and while he hated to decline, he simply couldn't bear being there even though he longed for his family during the holidays.

The case had stalled when Savannah Steadman-Teague conveniently slipped off for a couple of days to Tupelo for a Christmas flea market. But they'd sent the photo of the bracelet and she claimed she didn't know who it belonged to. The same claim Natalie and Maya had both made.

Tomorrow was Christmas Eve, and Gray Creek residents were in full swing gearing up for the annual Christmas Eve parade. The excitement sizzled in the atmosphere and tugged on his heart. Tuesday night, he and Poppy had brought the tree back to the B&B.

Beth had been hyperexcited about it and Delilah had been grateful. She managed to bring down some older ornaments and they had played Christmas music and decorated the tree together. Poppy had even sung along—a little off-key—to Christmas songs and had brought him hot chocolate then razzed him about putting ornaments of the same color too close together. And she called him a control freak.

She and Beth had chosen a star over an angel to top the tree. Poppy had really taken to Beth.

And sadly, Rhett had really taken to Poppy.

Now Rhett stood on the newly built front porch at the B&B waiting on Poppy to come down and start the day. Decorating the tree had been medicine for their foggy minds and tired bodies. He'd woken early feeling ready to tackle the day—the coffee and snickerdoodles for breakfast hadn't hurt either. His body ached and he was still sore, but his brain was all in and he was in a guns-blazing mood. Poppy deserved closure and peace. Deserved to fight the war inside her and win. It was a battle that he couldn't tag in on, but he could aid her on the investigative battlefield.

"You're gonna catch your death out here while staring into nothing." Poppy held a to-go cup of coffee, the steam pluming into the morning haze. "You must be in deep thought. Didn't even flinch when I walked out the front door." She cocked her head and shot him a quick grin—those were coming easier to her now. Her bangs hung thick across her brow, hiding her eyebrows but framing those gorgeous hazel eyes accented with long lashes. She wore a green turtleneck sweater and a pair of sleek black pants. She buttoned her coat and shivered. "I—"

"Hate the cold," they said in unison and she hooted.

"How'd you know?" she teased. "So what are you out here thinking?"

Nothing he wanted to reveal. "I'm thinking no one we talk to again is going to come forward. And we have no reason to make them." They had no concrete evidence. Only speculation.

"Because it's all we have. We've spent more time trying to save our bacon than finding leads."

Rhett pushed off the railing and motioned Poppy to take the porch steps first. "The last couple of nights have been quiet." They'd run into Ian Kirkwood the other night eating dinner, and while he didn't appear to have any noticeable marks or a limp, he wasn't being ruled out as a suspect. He also hadn't been thrilled to see them and he hadn't recognized the bracelet.

The interior of the car was colder than the outdoors. "I'd really like those seat warmers to kick in about now," Poppy said and slid her coffee into the cup holder by the console. She whipped out black leather gloves and slipped her slender fingers inside. "PS. I'm not really thrilled about returning to the Castlewood Mansion after nearly dying there."

He wasn't either, but that's where Savannah's office was located. He pulled onto the main road and headed for downtown.

"I was thinking about buying Beth a Christmas gift while we're on the Square. She's attached to the bunny but maybe she'd like a new dress for it. I don't know. And I feel like I owe Delilah something better than a sausage-and-cheese gift set. I hate those things."

Rhett snorted. "I kinda like 'em."

Poppy sipped her coffee. "You would. Well, I'll find something. See it and know it's right."

"The agency is already paying for the damage on her home."

Poppy groaned. "Nothing says Merry Christmas like a reimbursement check to pay for home repairs thanks to a killer trying to blow us to kingdom come. Let's also send them a congratulatory card for not ending up as collateral damage. Well done, Cordrays, you lived." She ended it with a fisted victory pump.

Rhett slowed down when he hit the main strip. "Done yet?"

"A thank-you card for not kicking us out?"

He frowned, but she was amusing. So that's what extra sleep did to her. Raised her snark game. Great.

Stopping at the stop sign, he frowned. It was a madhouse out today with crowded sidewalks and last-minute shoppers. Pushing through throngs of people for a Christmas gift that she would know when she saw it was not on his list of ways to have fun. It meant endless stores and endless lines. He'd almost rather be shot again. Definitely would rather jump off a train.

"Why can't you know what you want before you shop?"

She slurped her coffee. "Seeing is believing."

"What does that mean in the shopping context?" he asked, slightly irritated.

"I have no idea. Sounded good."

"No. It didn't."

She arched an eyebrow. "What bee flew up your tail-pipe this morning?"

He ignored her and huffed. Well, if they were stuck shopping, and were going to be at the B&B for Christmas, then Poppy ought to have something to open on Christmas morning. Didn't seem right for her to wake up without a gift. He didn't go home over the holidays, but Mom always mailed his presents. He'd never bought Poppy a gift before, but then they'd never spent a Christmas together.

And…and, well, against his better judgment he simply wanted to. "I'm gonna pass on shopping. Not that I don't want to buy them anything. I'll give you some cash."

"Way to do your part," she said with a slight snarl. "You're such a guy."

He turned up the holiday music. "I'm not insulted by that, you know."

She answered with a huff and silence. "I will take your cash, though."

He laughed and parked in front of the historic home that had nearly taken Poppy's life only days earlier. Poppy hesitated with her hand on the door handle.

"We'll stick to the first floor," he said, hoping his teasing hit its mark.

She pointed at him. "You better believe that." Inside, Savannah met them in the foyer. "Come on in my office. I won't offer for you to take a tour again. I'm mortified that someone would harm you, and here in my work space." She laid a hand on her chest and Rhett heard Poppy mutter under her breath.

"I'm sure."

They sat in Savannah's office. Déjà vu.

"I'm gonna cut to the chase. I've been abducted, choked, shot and chased. I'm over bedside manner," Poppy stated. "I know you smoked pot. I know you bought it from Linden Saddler. I know you were a real piece of work in high school."

Savannah opened her mouth as if to protest, but Poppy held up a hand and cut her off before she began. "I don't care that you've changed. Made amends. Decorate homes now or shop at flea markets. I don't care that your husband is a detective. I'm interested in your behavior in high school—whether or not you're proud of it—and I want to know why you lied about Dylan not having a crush on Cora when I have more than one credible witness stating that he did. I've had victims of your public humiliation schemes spill, so come clean."

Poppy leaned across the desk and gave Savannah the look that made grown men cry. She was the bulldog on the team. "Because so help me if you don't, I will make your mean-girl self look like Barbie. See, I'm pretty adept at getting my way too."

A flash of the mean girl shot through Savanah's eyes but she quickly composed that hot temper. No. Savannah Steadman-Teague did not like Poppy's threats. If only she was wise enough to know that they weren't threats at all. Poppy was proclaiming promises. Ones she would absolutely follow through on. The woman could terrify a person with a cold look, and he found it rather impressive.

Savannah clearly calculated and weighed her options, then she tossed her long blond hair behind her shoulder. "I don't think you need to go that far. I didn't tell you about my behavior in high school because it's irrelevant to your case. I didn't have anything to do with Cora's death. And mostly I'm ashamed of the behavior. So I don't usually go touting my former ways."

Poppy continued to stare. "Tell me about the pot. How did Cora get it?"

Savannah toyed with an ink pen, then sighed. "I could tell you who gave it to her but it would still be irrelevant."

Rhett scooted closer to Poppy in case she decided to come across the table at Savannah's evasiveness. "What would be relevant?" Rhett asked.

"Who gave the marijuana to Linden."

Poppy balled her hand into a fist. "I'm not interested in drug suppliers."

Savannah squirmed. "I think you should be. The pot was Maya's. But she didn't purchase it, and that may be relevant."

"How so?" Poppy asked.

Savannah rapidly blinked and heaved a sigh. "Maya was seeing the supplier on the down low. But she wasn't the only girl being supplied—if you get my drift."

"I'd rather get a solid statement. Who supplied the drugs and why is it relevant?"

Savannah leaned forward. "Mr. Simms. And it's important because he was known to take interest in some of the girls and that included pot if they wanted it— for free."

Poppy's face paled and she stared at Savannah wide-eyed. Linden Saddler had said that Maya never bought drugs. He knew she'd been getting them for free from his supplier. "Are you saying Mr. Simms—the science teacher and club sponsor—was having inappropriate relationships with students? With Cora?"

"I'm saying he had a thing with Maya, and he appeared to have an interest in Cora too, according to Maya. She was jealous. Simms was *her* older man. She thought it was actually going to go somewhere."

Poppy stood. "If I find out you're lying…"

"I'm not. I never thought Mr. Simms hurt Cora. If I did, I would have told. But the thing is Dylan said he saw something. Mr. Simms kept Cora after class the Friday she disappeared. He didn't overhear anything, but when Cora came out of class she was upset."

"And you didn't think this was pertinent back then

or when we were here days ago?" Poppy said, her voice raised.

"Back then I didn't think at all. Because I didn't care. And I didn't say anything days ago because I didn't think about it until you brought up the pot. I don't know if it was nefarious. He may have propositioned Cora and that upset her, or it could have been about her grades. Or anything. I don't know."

Mr. Simms. Drug distributor who was taking advantage of students—and had possibly been involved in Cora's death.

Poppy blew through the front door of the Victorian house, and the blast of wintry air did nothing to cool the blazing fire raging through her. She was no Doc Holliday. She was Wyatt Earp and this law dog was coming for Solomon Simms. With a vengeance.

Rhett caught up with her down the sidewalk. "Poppy..." he warned.

"If he so much as laid one finger on my sister, Rhett..." She couldn't even voice her thoughts. So many emotions.

He caught her arm at the car and forced her to face him. "Then we will bring him down. He will never see the light of day again. But we have to do it by the book so he goes away. One mistake and we're done. Look me in the eye and tell me you'll go by the book. This isn't a standoff at high noon. It's measured steps. Due process. Getting it right."

He was right. One hundred percent, but she didn't want to take measured steps. She wanted to barrel in there, guns blazing and aim and fire. And she'd lose.

Lose everything she wanted to bring to her family and to Cora. To herself.

Thankful for Rhett, she stepped into his space and touched his cheek. "I know. You're spot on." Laying her hand against his cheek brought her complete solace and opened up some breathing room. Having a constant, reliable person on her side was a good thing.

Maybe if she brought justice to Cora she could allow herself one good thing.

Maybe.

He covered her hand with his, soft and warm, and lowered their laced fingers to his chest. "I want you to know that I'm writing this down. Poppy Holliday told me I was right."

She laughed. This was no laughing matter but she needed it, and he seemed to not only know it, but to anticipate her needs and follow through to provide for her. It was bittersweet. "Write down anything you want. But you have no witnesses."

"Way to ruin the moment." His lips twitched and she had a mind to peck those lips, but she refrained. Now wasn't the time. It likely would never be the right time.

"Let's go find Simms."

"Oh, you better believe it." He released her hand and hurried to the driver's side. "I'm going to take the lead with him, Poppy. I need you to restrain yourself. We also have to consider the possibility that Maya was jealous that Simms paid attention to Cora. She knew Dylan had been too. Maybe she thought she would take care of Cora coming after her man and Savannah's. And we're still looking at Natalie."

"As if Cora would give Mr. Simms the time of day or respond to his proposition if there was one."

"No, but Maya may not have known that and she'd been trained by the best mean girl around." He sighed. "Restraint. Okay?"

That wasn't going to be easy. But again, he was right. "Fine," she said testily but he grinned, figuring out her gruff annoyance with him was all an act. Did he know it always had been?

By the time they drove into Solomon Simms's modest subdivision, Poppy was champing at the bit. Simms's car was under the carport. Good.

"Pop, I mean it. Rapport. That's what we need. Less aggression. If you can't do that, then you need to stay in the car."

Rhett knew when to be soft and tender and when to call her on her wayward ways. She hated it and needed it all at the same time. No one had ever been so...knowing of her. Words teetered on the tip of her tongue. Words she'd never spoken to a man who wasn't her brother. A tidal wave of panic crashed over her.

"What's wrong?" he asked. She couldn't hide anything from Mr. Observant. His knowledge of her only intensified her fear.

"Nothing," she choked out. "I'll be on my best behavior."

"That's not reassuring. Your best behavior is dismal." He grinned. "Yeah, I said dismal."

She had to get out of this car right now. Right this second, or she was going to throw herself into his arms and say and do something that she might or might *not* regret. Either way it was wrong. "I'll be cool as a cube," she said, intending to frustrate him with another annoying idiom.

But instead he reached out and ran his fingers under

her bangs, sliding them from her eyes. "It's cucumber, Agent Holliday," he murmured. "Cool as a cucumber, and we're in this together." He nodded once softly, then removed his touch. She wasn't warm; she was burning. All the way to her bones, and ready to profess thoughts she had no business even flirting with.

Did he have her number on the confusing phrases? How? She was losing every defense she knew to throw out.

He opened the car door and she followed him to the long gray porch. He rang the doorbell and a dog barked. Solomon Simms opened the door and a little Westie barked like a menacing giant. The man didn't deserve such a cute puppy. A stray thought went through her mind that when he went to prison, she'd rescue the dog.

"Agents." He opened the door, motioned them inside and then quieted his yapper by scooping it up. "Come in."

His house was tidy and decorated in masculine tones. Nothing fancy. But nothing that revealed he was a creeper. People were adept at keeping secrets. Rhett gave her the stern eye and stepped forward as Simms motioned for them to sit on the love seat. He sat across from them on the recliner. She noticed, at a closer look, dark purple circles under his eyes and he seemed a little peeved. His dog curled up in his lap.

"Are you feeling okay, Mr. Simms?" Rhett asked. Always polite. Garnering trust.

"So why are you here today?" he asked, evasively. Everyone loved evading their questions. Whatever. His personal health was none of their business.

"It's come to our attention that you had an illegal affair with Maya Marx while she was in high school. It's also come to our attention you grew pot and distributed it through Linden Saddler. So can you clear some stuff up for us?" Rhett asked.

He shifted uncomfortably in his chair.

"Did you have untoward intentions regarding my sister?" Poppy softly asked.

Simms inhaled deeply and stroked his little companion. "Any interest I expressed in Cora was for her impressive scientific mind. She could have received a full academic scholarship. Been something great."

Poppy choked back tears. Cora would never have that chance now. "Maya? The marijuana?"

He looked at his dog as he spoke. "I was twenty-seven at that time. No excuse for my relationship with Maya Marx, but she was the only one I had any kind of personal relationship with. It wasn't *girls*, plural. Only Maya."

"Did Maya think you had a personal interest in Cora?" Rhett asked and leaned forward on his knees. "It's possible that she hurt Cora."

Simms swallowed hard. "I guess it really doesn't matter now."

"What doesn't?" Poppy asked.

"The secrets. The years of secrets and lies." His voice was distant. Regretful even. "I loved Maya. She was seventeen—older than the rest but held back due to some earlier problems in school. But that is neither here nor there concerning Cora. Maya came to me the night Cora died. Hysterical. Banging on my door around 1:00 a.m. Babbling incoherently. It was a mistake. It wasn't supposed to happen."

Poppy's gut knotted. "What wasn't supposed to happen?"

Simms looked her in the eye and slowly shook his head. "After I got her calmed down, she told me that Savannah found out Dylan was going to break up with her to ask out Cora. Savannah had concocted some elaborate plan to derail it. She befriended Cora and gained her trust by asking her to hold the bag of weed. It wasn't Maya's. I would know. I gave it to Linden specifically for Savannah."

He was admitting to growing and selling pot. "Are you still dealing?"

"No. I sold it back then to help pay off student loans only. That's why I picked Linden to help. He wanted to save for a business. We weren't in it to build a drug empire."

Oh, well then, it must be okay to sell drugs if the reason was noble. Poppy refrained from an eye roll.

"Now I only grow it for medicinal purposes. I'm dying of cancer. I was in Atlanta for treatment. It's terminal. Treatment slows it but won't put me into remission."

Now he wanted to come clean because he was dying and had nothing to lose. But what about all those years ago when they grieved? When they were awake, sick, wondering if she'd been kidnapped and trafficked somewhere without her meds? Poppy clenched her teeth and balled her fists until her nails bit into her flesh.

"Please continue," Rhett said, his jaw tick showing his own depth of restraint.

"Once she gathered Cora's trust, she made a plan with Ian Kirkwood."

Guess he wasn't at the movies alone after all.

"She invited Cora out that night to a little get-together at the Weaverman property. Told her that Ian would pick her up and bring her. Which I assume he did. She was there."

That's why she sneaked out. To meet a boy her parents didn't know. A boy they didn't know wasn't allowed to drive them anywhere, and Poppy had known that Cora liked Dylan and would question why another boy was picking her up and where she was going.

"The plan—" he paused and closed his eyes a moment "—was to make it appear like Cora was into Ian when Dylan arrived by seeing them together in the back seat of Ian's car."

Poppy fumed. "What did he do to her?"

"It wasn't like that. He was only going to make it look like they were kissing in the back seat, but Savannah knew that Cora would never do that."

"Did she force her?"

"No. She took a sedative from her mother that was only supposed to make Cora groggy or even sleep a bit. That way they could plant her in the back seat and make it appear that way. When Dylan saw that Cora wasn't into him like he was into her, then he wouldn't want Cora."

There were some holes in the plot, but teenagers rarely thought things out. Cora could have told Dylan later that she didn't remember or that she was drugged, and knowing Savannah and her friends, Dylan would have known something was up. He could have beaten it out of Ian unless Ian had something to gain by Dylan not liking Cora. Maybe Cora for himself. Or Savannah might have had something on Ian and still did today. Maybe he'd gone into the military to escape this sordid night.

"But whatever they gave her resulted in a seizure

and she died." Simms had the decency to look at the floor and pause.

Poppy clamped the inside of her bottom lip to keep from falling into a puddle on the floor.

"I don't think they knew she had a condition, and they certainly wouldn't have thought the sleeping pill could cause an adverse reaction due to the meds she may have been on. I surmised that's what happened and that her death was accidental."

"It was malicious," Poppy hissed. "Over a stupid boy." More than anything, she wanted to run off to a corner and break down and cry for her sister's life that was cut short. But she had a job to do, so she pulled herself together as much as she could. "Finish what you know."

"They panicked. Dylan wanted to go to the police, but Ian, Natalie and Savannah talked him out of it. They... Well, you know where they put her. But Natalie or Savannah or both of them—I don't know really— lost a piece of jewelry in the well and freaked out."

That explained the bracelet. Everyone was lying about who it belonged to. May be why Zack paused so long when Poppy had texted the photo to him. He'd recognized it as his wife's.

"Ian told them no one was going to look down there ever. So they left, but it wrecked Maya."

Poppy gritted her teeth so she wouldn't say anything about Maya at least being alive while Cora was not.

"I'm so sorry," he said.

"You're sorry? You kept the secret because not only did you grow and distribute the marijuana, but you were having an illegal relationship with Maya and needed to protect yourself." Her disgust couldn't be hidden and she didn't care.

Rhett stood. "We'll have to confirm all this with Maya. She'll probably go to prison."

Simms nodded. "I suppose I might be going too."

Except he was terminal and it didn't matter to him. He was already a dead man walking.

"Do you know if Dylan tried to come clean at all over the years?" Rhett asked.

"Maya said on the anniversary of her death he would go out to the Weaverman property. Sometimes she met him there. Sometimes he was alone and he talked a few times of turning them in, but he was in a practice with Natalie and she was married to his brother."

Nice reason to make him keep his trap shut, and to keep tabs on him through the shared practice. Savannah had married a cop and it could ruin his career if he found out—and Savannah's. Ian would lose his business.

But then they'd found her body. Dylan must have either wanted to come forward and one of them killed him, or he couldn't handle the repercussions and committed suicide—or maybe he did drink himself into a stupor and died driving out there or trying to drive to the sheriff's office. Unless someone confessed or the trace evidence came back with something solid, they may never know.

Why would Savannah give up Simms and Maya tonight knowing it would connect back to her and her part in all this? "Does anyone know you're terminal?"

"No. I just found out myself."

Savannah must have been banking on Simms keeping his secrets and lies and his mouth shut. She didn't know he had nothing to lose by telling the truth anymore. Now that it had backfired, she still had the upper hand. All they had to do was call Simms a liar; his reason for it wouldn't matter. All they needed for a hung jury was a reasonable doubt, and if they kept their alibis and stuck to the same story, they'd get off scot-free.

"We'll see ourselves out."

Rhett stayed silent until they were inside the car. "He's going to give Maya a heads-up—you know that."

"Let's hope Maya wants to talk too. Clear her conscience."

TWELVE

As much as Poppy wanted to make a beeline for Maya Marx, she was at the clinic. Having Natalie nearby wouldn't play in their favor. They needed her alone and uninfluenced by another accessory to the crime. But they could talk to Ian Kirkwood again. Shake him up. Shake something loose. He had a lot to lose, so she wasn't banking on honesty—especially if he was the one trying to shut her down permanently.

Rhett agreed and they kept what they knew to themselves. Courtesy toward Detective Teague was one thing, but letting him know that it had grown to this magnitude meant he could wreck their investigation if he tipped off Savannah that Simms was terminal and had spilled the beans. They needed to play each of these people off the others. Simms's condition and what they'd been told had to stay quiet for now. If the suspects didn't know the confession came from him, they'd assume it came from someone in their clique, and they might turn on each other for a better deal.

But Rhett hated playing dirty.

"I played nice. I restrained myself," Poppy said. "Now it's time to play it my way. We have the upper hand. We can play these guys off one another. We only need one of them to corroborate what Simms said."

"I had a feeling you'd say that." He nodded. "Take the lead, Bulldog. Close this case."

They pulled into the parking lot at Ian Kirkwood's place of business and went inside only to find they'd just missed him. They were told he had to run out for a few errands and said he'd be back in an hour or two.

Or the phone tree had already begun to shake and he was running.

"Now what?" Poppy asked as they marched back to the car and got inside.

"We tip them off if we meet up with Maya and Natalie together. So let's do this," Rhett said. "Let's do nothing for a minute. You need to process—not as an investigator but a family member who's had a bomb dropped."

"Bad choice of words, Wallace." Poppy smirked, knowing once again Rhett was right. Her mind was a whirlwind of thoughts all jumbled with her emotions. She needed to sort them out and make sense of them, and she needed to call Tack. It wasn't time to share this information with her parents. They needed more proof, but Simms had no reason to lie. But Tack was also a Texas Ranger working unsolved homicides, and he needed to hear the story going down.

"My bad. Okay, how about we go get some lunch, then you can do that shopping and take some time alone at the B&B wrapping gifts."

Poppy rubbed her hands along her thighs. "And what are you going to do while I shop?"

"Anything else. Probably catch Colt up on the case." He backed out of Kirkwood's parking lot. Maybe their heads-up could play to their advantage after all. They'd panic and someone would come forward, admit it and embellish what had happened. Beg for a deal. Identify the bracelet. All they needed was one to tell the truth, or even half truths. They could work that against them too.

They chose a little sandwich shop for lunch and ordered club sandwiches and tomato-basil soup. Poppy didn't realize how hungry she was until she tasted the tangy tomatoes. But her mind was a whirlpool of thoughts. If Savannah gave Cora the sedative, then she was going down for manslaughter and she could get all the others on accessory-after-the-fact. But what about Dylan?

"I know what you're thinking. Best way to get every last one of them." He picked a piece of bacon from his sandwich and took a bite.

"I am." Talking in this little but crowded establishment wasn't an option. "Every last one of them." She echoed his words and finished her soup.

After lunch and splitting a huge pecan brownie, they left the cozy warmth of the café for the blustery temperature outdoors. Snow flurries swirled and a toddler was catching them on her tongue. "I'm going into the doll shop three stores down. Let's meet over there at that cart selling warm drinks in two hours."

He nodded and she weaved through the crowd. Killers were out there and Cora was dead, and she was shopping for a little outfit for Beth's bunny. Seemed off kilter, but also the right thing. Should she be taking a simple pleasure in buying a gift? At one time she wouldn't have even thought about it.

She'd wanted her life to be miserable to prove to Cora how sorry she was. Something had shaken loose, though. And Poppy had a sick feeling she knew what it was. Something she didn't want to happen, had never intended to happen.

After purchasing a pair of pink-and-blue pajamas with little hearts for Beth's bunny, she found a boutique and bought a matching pink gown with one big heart on the front for Beth. Then she found a holiday candle made from soy for Delilah.

There was still time before she had to meet up with Rhett, so she perused all the shops and found a perfect present for him. After all, they would be spending Christmas together. Unless they could get confessions beforehand, and then she'd be spending Christmas alone. She could still leave him with a gift if that happened. He'd be spending Christmas alone too.

She bought him a little plaque that said I Am Silently Correcting Your Grammar. Maybe she'd mark out "Grammar" and add "Idioms." Chuckling, she laid the plaque on the counter and paid for it, then tucked it in the bag with all her other presents.

After meeting up with Rhett, they headed back to the B&B. She borrowed scissors and tape from Delilah and went upstairs to her room to wrap presents and call Tack. He answered on the first ring.

"You okay?" he asked.

"Yes. We have a lead. I feel it in my gut this is it, but we need some confessions." She rolled out the red-and-green Christmas paper she'd purchased. When was the last time she bought a Christmas gift? She cut along the faint lines and cradled the cell phone between her neck and ear.

"Don't beat it out of them," he teased.

Poppy laughed. "No, that's what you'd do, you roughneck cowboy." She cut along the marked lines. "No worries. Rhett won't let me knock anybody around."

"How's he holding up?"

"Ever the Superman." And ever the Clark Kent too. "He's an excellent agent and he's got a backbone. He's no daisy."

Tack chuckled. "I hear something in that voice of yours. Little more than admiration, Pops. Y'all got something goin'?"

Did they? No. But was there something there? For her? Yes. But she was working on that. "We're colleagues and you know how things worked out with Liam."

"I know he was a jerk who thought the world revolved around him and he was a strong-armer. I've met Wallace. He's a good egg, Pops. Be good for you."

"Yeah, well, I got enough protein in my diet. No matter, I wouldn't be good for him. Besides, he's made it clear that I'm not his type and he'd never ask me out." She was too much of a wild card. Well, he was too much of a stiff shirt. Or stuffed shirt. Whatever.

"So there is something there. Poppy, listen to me. Don't let love slip away if you can hold on to it. Okay? I'm not always the mushy guy—"

"You are the furthest thing from mush unless punching me to show love counts," she teased, but Tack was what people called a man's man. There was nothing flowing through his veins but hot blood and testosterone.

"Yeah, well…maybe that's my cross to bear. It's not yours," he said with power in his voice. "Do you hear me? You don't need to carry an unnecessary burden. Cora wouldn't want you to be miserable because she's gone. That kid forgave anyone for anything. Even that time I accidentally threw her from my handle bars when a dog ran out in front of us. I felt terrible when she broke her arm because of it. She'd broken enough bones from seizures. I could barely look her in the eye, but when I made it to her bedside she wrapped her good arm around me and told me it wasn't my fault. And her death isn't yours."

"What if it is, though? What if we argued and she sneaked out due to something I said? And I couldn't follow her because I was grounded for taking the blame for pot that wasn't mine."

"If that's what happened, I'd say it's still not your fault. She knew right from wrong and made her choice. Don't you think it's time to forgive yourself? She's not in pain. She's in a way better place than us. No more seizures. Would I rather have her here? Yes, but that's purely selfish. I promise she's not angry anymore because you yelled at her and told her she ought to be rebellious for once in her life. And if what's keepin' you from a decent relationship and finding happiness is that you think you don't deserve it, you're wrong. Get over it. Don't create more regrets."

His words were far from soft or eloquent, but that wasn't Tack's approach. And the way he put it made sense. Cora wasn't angry or bitter or regretful. She was pain free, sorrow free and feeling nothing but joy in the presence of God. "I appreciate the pep talk. Truly. But I don't date colleagues."

"You haven't dated the right colleague. If this guy puts up with your hard head and malarkey, then maybe there's more there. Not many would put up with your smart mouth and bossy attitude." His voice held love and teasing.

"Yeah, yeah. Hey, I heard Chelsey was in Texas for a few days. You seen her?"

"Why are you bringing her up in the context of dating?" She wasn't. Well…maybe she was. "I'm not."

"Mmm…she's fine. I've seen her a few times." The clipped tone meant he wasn't saying any more and she needed to drop it.

"I have to go. We're going to Maya's to get confirmation about Simms. Hopefully."

"She might crack. Go the route of easing her conscience. Doing the right thing. That might work better than strong-arming her."

She huffed. "Yes, Mr. Texas Ranger. Give my love to the fam." She hung up before he could tell her she ought to fly home for Christmas.

After tucking her gifts under the bed, she knocked on Rhett's bedroom door. He opened it with his jacket over his arm. "Ready?"

"Yep."

She followed him downstairs. The house was quiet except for Christmas music playing in the private living space for Delilah and Beth. "I got their presents wrapped," Poppy said as she slipped on her coat and they stepped out into the snow. It was sticking. A few pieces of grass poked through but the way the snow was coming down all fat and flaky, it would be a nice and unusual white Christmas.

Snow was beautiful. Too bad it had to be cold.

"Delilah said that if we can't leave, we're welcome to have dinner on both Christmas Eve and Christmas with her and Beth. It's just them. No immediate family."

That was sad. At least Poppy had family, even though she rarely saw them under the circumstances.

Maya's little brick craftsman sat farther back from the road in a rural area of Gray Creek. Her car was in the drive and a truck was parked behind it. The light was on inside. Good sign.

They parked and climbed the gray concrete steps to the wide porch. A meager Christmas tree twinkled with multicolored lights, and Christmas music played. Not exactly the atmosphere Poppy expected for a woman who'd been given a heads-up that the cops were on to her. Maybe she hadn't been warned by Simms.

Rhett knocked and got no answer. He rang the doorbell then knocked louder. Nothing.

"I'll go around back," Poppy said. She hopped down the porch stairs and rounded the side of the house as a figure came barreling out of the back. "Stop!" Poppy hollered and drew her weapon, trying to get a good look at his face, but he was running away from her. Brown hair. Same build as her own attacker. "Rhett!"

The man kept running and Poppy pursued as Rhett caught up. "Who is it?"

"Not sure."

"I'll keep chase. You go find Maya. He's running for a reason."

Poppy pivoted and raced back to the house, going through the screened-in porch into the kitchen.

Maya lay on the kitchen floor.

Dead.

Rhett pursued the man through the woods. He was sick of running in and out of woods. He hoped the next case would be in the city. Full of traffic and not a tree in sight.

Sirens wailed in the distance. Poppy had called the police and probably an ambulance. Was Maya alive?

He closed in on the killer and tackled him to the ground. "You have the right to remain silent," he said, grabbing his cuffs from his belt and sliding the bracelets on his bloody wrists, then patting him down before rolling him over.

Ian Kirkwood.

"I didn't do it."

"No? Just decided to get bloody, then take a jog through the woods?" He finished Mirandizing him and hauled him to his feet. "Didn't do what, by the way?"

"I didn't stab Maya." He shifted under Rhett's hold on his jacket collar. "I'm not going to run again."

"No, you definitely are not." Rhett let go but pointed his gun on him. "Why run at all?"

"Because when I saw you and Agent Holliday get out of the car I knew you'd think I'd done it. I panicked."

Likely story. This bunch had been lying through their teeth since the beginning. Nothing out of his mouth was believable.

"I need to get this blood off my hands, man!"

"I imagine you have more than one person's blood on your hands." As they approached the house, an ambulance, sheriff's marked units and both Detectives Banner and Teague were on the scene.

Monty came racing toward Ian, and Rhett jumped in front to block the blow the detective was about to deal. "Hey. Hey."

Teague held Monty off. "Don't be stupid, Banner. We got him. He'll pay."

"For what?" Ian hollered. "I didn't kill her."

Teague raised a skeptical eyebrow. "Innocent men don't run." He tugged and pulled Monty away, assuring him of justice. But Rhett knew justice wasn't always served. Not in this life.

Poppy stepped outside, the wind blowing her hair like something out of a movie. The hot tough detective in her blue latex gloves and a chip on her shoulder. His heart thundered and he reminded himself this was a crime scene. She had him spinning out of control, though, and it was terrifying.

She met up with him and turned her hard expression to Ian. "I'll see you at the sheriff's office."

Rhett shoved him in the back of Detective Teague's unmarked car and slammed the door, then went inside to the scene. CSI were photographing and processing the house, as well as Ian's truck.

Poppy knelt by Maya's body. "No sign of a struggle. Coffee was freshly brewed and enough for more than one person. Two mugs were out. One on the table and one unused. She thought her attacker had come as friend not foe. If they got into an argument over Cora or the latest news Simms gave us, then I think there would have been a struggle of some kind. A piece of furniture tossed. My guess is he got up to fix his coffee and grabbed the knife from the block, and it was done before she had a chance to register she was being attacked. It was quick and efficient."

Rhett's stomach roiled. Maya may have taken part in Cora's alleged accidental death but she didn't deserve to be butchered. "Like a hunter or a skilled soldier. Quick cut. Ian hunts, was in the military, and he had blood all over his hands."

Poppy sighed, long and tired. "Let's see if we can get him to talk without a lawyer. You do it. I'll botch it. I'm too..." She burst up and out the door so fast it made his head spin.

He found her alone under a huge tree by the side of the house, eyes closed and head upward. Snow dotted her long lashes.

"We're going to get to the truth, Poppy. We're close."

"I feel like I'm fighting a losing battle. I don't have Dylan's story or Maya's. I have whatever fabrication Ian, Natalie and Savannah are going to give me."

He crossed to the tree and grasped her shoulders. She opened her eyes, blinking away the tiny drops of snow. "Ian is picking them off one by one. The women will be scared. They'll want to talk."

"And say what? Ian did it all. Simms is lying. We have no proof now. The key players are all dead."

Rhett framed her pink cheeks, cold from the temperature. "I know. I know." She melted against him, and seemed to find rest in his embrace. It brought satisfaction and a tremor of anxiety. He liked being her soft place to land. Liked that she trusted him to be a shelter. A safe haven. Without thinking it through carefully, he drew her even closer, cocooning her and resting his head on hers. "I'm sorry you're going through this. I wish there was something more I could do."

Poppy raised her head, and her nose brushed his. Her lips were so close. Pulse spiking and heat chasing away the chill, he peered into her eyes and saw the questions, hope and sincerity. Pure. Intense.

Deliberately he eased down until his lips touched hers. Soft and sweet. It ignited a fire clear to his toes, and he tested the waters to see if she was as willing as she appeared. Her arms slipped around his waist, her hands resting on his back. She stole his breath and infused him with such power, all in one tender kiss.

Poppy was as strong in her kiss as she was in her job. As unpredictable and full of surprises as she was in life. It was like getting a taste of something delicious and craving more.

Finally, she broke away and left his heart gaping open wide. Left his mind scrambled and dazed, and yet he'd never felt more grounded. More in control.

"I wasn't expecting that," she said through a ragged breath.

"I guess I'm not as predictable as you thought." Or as he thought. He licked his bottom lip and breathed deep to bring down his heart rate. He wasn't expecting that either—not the emotion. Not the connection.

She grinned. "I suppose not." Then her grin faltered and she blew out a heavy breath.

"Just another emotional moment?" he asked, worried she'd say yes but also concerned she'd say no. That's what she'd claimed in her room when they'd almost kissed before. That she'd have kissed anyone. But she wasn't kissing anyone.

She'd been in Rhett's arms just a second ago.

Panic replaced her calm expression. "I don't know. You said yourself—"

"I said a lot of things." But he didn't know either.

"Like you don't date colleagues. Just kiss them, then?" she asked in a lighter tone, then sobered. "I dated a colleague back when I worked for the SO in Desoto County and it ended badly. The truth is, Rhett, all my relationships end badly. And I didn't care. Not even a little. But if we—if it—I'd care," she whispered. "I'd care more than a little. So… I can't think about that right now. I'm sorry."

He nodded. At least she wasn't being brutal or throwing up her biting defense mechanism. She was being purely honest and he respected that because he wasn't sure either. He had strict rules. Control. Structure. Could he toss all that out for the way she made him feel? Was it just about the way she made him feel? He had things to sort out too. "I understand. The timing is bad right now."

"It might not ever be better, Rhett. I don't know if we'd work."

He wasn't sure they would either, but as partners on the job, they worked. "Maybe not."

"Probably not."

The blow was suffocating. But Poppy was thinking clearer than he was. "You're right."

She snickered but it was full of disappointment. "I can't believe it. You say I'm right and no one is here to witness it." Motioning with her head toward the house, she said, "We have a job to do."

He followed her to the car and drove to the sheriff's office with little conversation. There wasn't much to say.

Inside the SO, Detective Teague and Sheriff Pritchard were interviewing Ian Kirkwood over the murder of Maya Marx. Detective Banner stood in the room with the two-way mirror, a scowl on his face. "He's not copping to it, but he admits picking up the knife in shock. Said she was dead when he got there. I don't believe him."

Neither did Rhett, but how did one force the hand

of a killer who knew how to keep a secret and take out those who could tell a different tale?

Poppy frowned and left the room, then knocked on the interview room door. Sheriff Pritchard rose and opened it, then he motioned Detective Teague out and Poppy entered. Rhett followed her inside.

"I didn't kill Cora. I didn't kill Maya," Ian recited as if he'd been practicing the words.

"Why were you at Maya's?"

"I told them and I'll tell you. I went by there because my dog has allergies and she had grabbed me some Apoquel—for dog allergics. But when I got there, she was dead. I freaked out. I checked for a pulse and tried compressions but she was gone. Yes, I picked up the knife. I wasn't thinking."

"Did you see anyone on the road passing you? She hadn't been dead long when you arrived," Poppy said as if she believed him.

"No."

"Did you know that she and Solomon Simms were having an illegal affair when you were in high school?"

His face blanched. "Yes. I knew. But not back then. I found out later, when she was about twenty and they were dating. They've been on and off again all these years. Does he even know? They were together the last couple of days."

Had Maya gone to Atlanta with Simms for his treatment? Rhett turned and looked toward the mirror. Did Monty know that Maya was with Simms? And if so… was that second cup of coffee his?

"Did she say where they were?"

Ian must have caught on that Monty was on the other side of the window listening. He glanced at the window and sighed. "Bed and breakfast to celebrate his recent remission. He had cancer. Maya told me—he doesn't know I know. But he's in remission now and that was the celebration."

They couldn't call to see if he'd been in Atlanta's cancer center or call a doctor because of HIPPA. Why would Simms lie about terminal cancer? Why give up Maya and her friends if he was going to live and they were together?

Unless she'd told him it was over.

Could Simms be playing them all somehow? And why? What was his end game?

THIRTEEN

Poppy sat at the dining room table at the B&B drinking coffee and overcome with exhaustion. It was Christmas Eve and they'd worked most of the day. Ian Kirkwood never admitted to killing Maya but wouldn't take a polygraph. Probably because of all the other things he'd done.

Solomon Simms had been given the news about Maya and he'd actually cried. He denied Ian's claims, but the fact he wouldn't let them see his medical records to prove it one way or the other left an unsettled feeling in her gut. So many lies. So many deceptions going on with so many people. The truth had long been blurred, and Poppy wasn't sure what to believe. Simms didn't look frail but he didn't exactly look well either.

The investigation of Maya's homicide wasn't in their hands, so they hadn't been able to interview Detective Monty Banner. He had motive, if she'd been seeing Simms in secret. Detective Teague was conducting that end of things, and he wasn't at all thrilled that his wife was in the middle of this. After her tough talk with Savannah, Teague had been less courteous. That was fair. Poppy had all but called his wife a liar and all-around vile person.

They'd just finished Christmas Eve dinner, and Delilah wouldn't let either of them help with the cleanup. Instead they'd sat at the table and played Candyland with Beth, drank coffee and ate too much pecan pie. Now Beth had gone to lie down and Rhett excused himself to call his sister.

It was almost time for the Gray Creek Christmas Eve parade. The town was all abuzz about it, and Beth had talked nonstop about eating popcorn and drinking hot chocolate while watching the floats come down Main Street and having her picture taken with Santa. The thought of one more bite or swig of sugar roiled Poppy's stomach, and she had no clue what she would ask Santa for if she accompanied Beth for pictures. She'd probably ask him to point her to the killer and help her solve Cora's case. Too bad Santa had no real ability to grant wishes or requests.

She wasn't sure God would answer her prayers either. It had been so long since she'd even prayed to Him. But she offered up a silent request anyway. Expected silence in return.

Which reminded her of yesterday's kiss. She and Rhett had been silent about that, but every time she thought of it, which was often, her belly dipped and her heart fluttered. She'd never once in her life been kissed the way Rhett kissed her.

The thought of it tingled her lips and kicked her heart rate up a notch. She ran her teeth along her bottom lip as if to try and scrape away the sensation. It hadn't even been so much about the way he kissed. It had felt like he'd humbled himself in it, to serve her and reveal beautiful truths about herself.

She was worth his time, devotion and effort.

She was cherished. Respected. Treasured.

How was it possible that she'd felt safe and secure in his kiss when it had been anything but safe, unencumbered by structure? Led by instinct. He'd tasted like adventure, the uncertainty thrilling. He'd revealed he was much more than routine and rules. He was unpredictable and audacious. Strong and secure. Trustworthy. Wild but careful with his kiss.

In that unhurried moment, she'd been content and felt real joy for the first time since Cora died, but it had also petrified her. She made a mess out of relationships and one with Rhett would be no different. Then she'd lose what little of him she held.

Tack's words had been rolling around her heart. Cora was happy now. Free.

She would want Poppy to be free of her guilt and shame and agony.

"What are you dreaming about?" Beth asked and sat next to her.

"I'm dreaming about wishes. Have you ever made a wish?" she asked.

Beth nodded. She was beautiful in her green-and-red sweater and black leggings. She laid her bunny on the table. In the morning, she'd have new pajamas for her sweet bunny. Or maybe Poppy would give them to her before bed so they could both wear their pajamas to sleep.

"I make birthday wishes every year, and I tell Santa my wish. I'm going to tell him my Christmas wish tonight too."

Delilah and Beth had invited her and Rhett to the Christmas Eve parade. Poppy glanced out the window. It had been snowing since yesterday morning and they now had three whole inches, which was like Snow-

mageddon in the South. It would be a beautiful night for
a lit-up parade of Christmas floats. Maybe she would
try to enjoy it. "What are you asking him for?"

"It's a surprise."

Poppy smiled. "Okay."

Rhett came downstairs, and Poppy's head went
fuzzy. She couldn't deny the effect he had on her.
He was dressed in trendy jeans and a red-and-black
Buffalo-check shirt with a gray cardigan over it. The
man was made for a magazine cover.

"I'm ready for the parade. What about you, Beth?" he
asked. Poppy loved the way his eyes lit up and warmed
when he was near Beth. Was there any part of Rhett
that wasn't admirable?

Delilah entered the dining room with Beth's coat
and they set off for the parade. The streets were already
lined with families eager to get a good view of the floats
and easy access to the candy that would be tossed to
the sides of the street. Christmas music played from the
speakers and Santa's Village was in full swing, gearing up for eager children giving last-minute wishes and
parents hoping for last-minute photos.

Other than the murders, Gray Creek was a wonderful place to live and raise a family.

"Who wants popcorn?" Rhett asked and Poppy
groaned. She didn't have room for anything else, even
if she could smell the buttery deliciousness from here.

"Me," Beth said.

"I'll be back in a minute," he said.

"Doubtful. Have you seen the line?" It was wrapped
around the center of the square. No one should want
popcorn that bad.

He winked and she tried to fight the gooey feeling.

"I'll be here waiting, saving your spot." About five minutes after Rhett left, her phone rang.

She didn't recognize the number. "Hello?" She covered one ear with her hand and pressed the phone harder to her other.

"Agent Holliday, it's Detective Teague."

"Hey. Do you have something?"

A long sigh filtered through the line. "Against my better judgment, my wife wants to talk to you. She's withheld information," he said and his irritation and disappointment filtered through the line. "I knew something was off with her since the body was discovered, but she wouldn't say a word."

"Until now?" Now that people in her inner circle were dropping like flies and Ian had been caught fleeing the scene. "She wants to make some kind of deal to rat out Ian, doesn't she?" It was only a matter of time before they began turning on one another out of fear and panic and self-preservation.

"She knows only the DA can offer a deal. She also knows what went down that night and it doesn't involve her, Natalie, Maya or Dylan. It doesn't even involve Ian, though he wasn't at the movies that night. He was with Savannah—" his voice broke "—but it does involve Solomon Simms."

These people deserved some kind of trophy for their ability to lie and hide the truth.

"Just…go easy on her, please? She's… I love her."

"If she tells the truth and she wasn't involved, then I'll do what I can and put in a good word to the DA. That's all I can promise. Fair?"

"Yeah. Yeah, that's fair."

"Where can I find her?" She didn't particularly want

to go back to the historical home. That place wigged her out now.

"Santa's Village. I'm the stupid Santa this year. We rotate. We can meet after. I'd like to be with her when you talk."

She might lose her nerve by then. "Let's meet now..." She blinked as she spotted Simms. What was he doing slinking around toward the back of the businesses? "Detective, I just spotted Solomon Simms. He's on the north side of Main Street beside the candle store. Talks will have to wait."

"He's dangerous, Agent. If you plan to do what I think, take Agent Wallace."

"Yeah," she mumbled, then hung up. Where was he going? She excused herself from Delilah. She wasn't going to confront but simply follow him, and she had no time to wait on Rhett. She'd lose Simms. Rhett knew she planned to take necessary risks. This was one.

It wasn't like she was some TV sleuth with no business tracking a villain. She was a trained agent with a gun on her hip, and she wasn't an idiot.

She stealthily moved through the crowd as Solomon Simms maneuvered toward the cobblestone street behind the shops. Was he dealing marijuana? Something even more nefarious? Keeping a safe distance, Poppy tracked him as he darted down the cobbled street by the shop. Cars were parked in every available space due to the parade; Christmas music rang out loud and the crowd was cheering even louder as colorful Christmas floats inched down the street with riders waving and tossing candy.

Simms ducked behind the building. Poppy waited a beat and moved in. She would catch this guy dead to rights, but when she turned the corner he was gone. Poof! Vanished.

She frowned and scanned the vacant street. Where could he have gotten to in such a hurry? Creeping along, she checked between cars. Gun in hand, she moved behind a tree. A scraping noise drew her attention but before she could investigate, something sharp pinched her neck and rough hands wrangled her behind the Dumpster.

Instantly her limbs turned to jelly and her insides became liquid, her muscles relaxing then numbing. Slowly but quickly. She was no longer able to grasp her gun, and it fell to the ground. She couldn't even wiggle her toes!

Panic gripped her as the realization dawned that she'd been injected with a paralyzing agent. Even blinking was becoming more difficult to manage.

"Is my job here done? I'm not into killing people."

Simms! He popped out from behind the car he'd been crouching behind. He'd lured her on purpose. Knew she'd see him and follow, giving the man who was now holding her a chance to get the drop on her with the drug. "I fed her the story about being terminally ill. Now, we had a bargain—don't forget to uphold your end. Don't you cross me," he warned the man who held Poppy captive.

He'd lied! Of course he had. They had all been lying through their teeth.

She was dragged farther, could feel the softness of her captor's coat, but her head wouldn't turn for her to see his face, and he hadn't spoken so she couldn't identify the voice. Horror filled her and she tried to cry out, to scream, but her lips wouldn't even move! Her throat had been paralyzed. A frenzy started inside and she wanted to claw out of her skin, burst away, but she was at this man's mercy. Simms walked away, leaving her in her captor's clutches.

"By now, you're probably wondering what's happening to you?"

That voice. She knew that voice!

"You've been drugged with succinylcholine. You probably don't know what that is. It's a neuromuscular blocking agent. Should be used in conjunction with anesthesia and a ventilating machine, but that's unnecessary for you. This is about keeping you from destroying everything I've worked for."

How had she done that?

"My mom was murdered when I was fourteen and my brother was eight. My dad became obsessed with finding the killer to the point of neglect. We had to live with my grandmother if we wanted to eat or have running water and heat. You have that same look in your eye. I heard you that night at the Weaverman property, talking about how you'd invade every nook and turn over every rock. I knew it. I knew you had to be stopped. Where other cops might give up searching, obsession would drive you on, and eventually you'd figure out what happened and destroy my life."

Poppy fought to make her muscles move, but there were only twitches and they were slowly dissipating.

"You've given me no choice." Something slid across the snow, as if he was dragging something. "By now you've realized you can hear and see and feel pain, but you can't move or talk or scream. Before too long, your lungs will be paralyzed, and you'll asphyxiate. I'd estimate you have an hour at most, maybe more, seeing you're rather muscular."

One hour and she would be dead.

"Then they'll find your body…or maybe not. Maybe you'll end up where your sister did and this time, they'll seal the top of the well since it's so dangerous. Be best. No one will even know you're down there. They've already done their search. No point going back."

He leaned down and his beard scraped against her cheek, his expensive cologne gagging her. His minty breath might as well have been a foul stench. "I guess time will tell."

Rhett inched through the line and listened as excited children chattered about Christmas gifts and which floats they were most excited to see. A parent reminded her children of the real meaning of Christmas and that Jesus was the biggest and greatest gift.

The kids agreed but didn't seem to believe it quite like their mother.

Had Rhett? Since Keith died, Christmas had changed for him. The joy was lost. The excitement and thrill of what it meant had vanished. Keith's death had inadvertently become the magnification of the holiday.

As "O Holy Night" played from the speakers, echoing words of the wondrous night of joy and hope, the lyrics struck him hard and in a way they hadn't before. He'd heard this carol—sung it even—half a dozen times this year at least, but as he listened to it now while a young mother tried to teach her children where the greatest hope and joy came from, the song reminded him of his lost hope and stolen joy. It had drowned that night in the icy waters. Grief snuffed out any thrill or excitement, and Rhett had buried the true meaning of Christmas.

It wasn't about toys, tradition or even loss.

It was about a loving God sending His Son to a lost and joyless world to rescue them.

A Keith-sized hole would always be inside him, but Jesus still saved even if He hadn't physically saved Keith that night. Keith was in heaven with Him.

Jesus still filled people with hope and joy. Rhett hadn't wanted to be filled with either of those. He'd assumed that living with the void was simply the way it was. What he deserved.

But Christmas was still a time to celebrate truth.

Rhett had changed after tragedy altered his life. What happened that holy night had not.

The backs of his eyes burned.

"Mama, I love Jesus, but I love my toys too," the little boy said and nudged his sister to respond.

She frowned at her brother, then broke out in a cheesy grin, revealing two gaps where her top front teeth should be. "Jesus is big in my heart. And a puppy will be little in my arms!"

Their mother grinned, fully amused and proud and slightly exasperated.

Was his mother proud? Rhett never showed up to celebrate the birth of Christ or that Jesus was the giver of life. He was too busy mourning and magnifying death.

The little girl turned and looked up at him. "Do you know the reason for the season, mister?"

Rhett's eyes continued to burn, but he nodded. "I do. I really do."

"And what are you asking Santa for? Can big people ask Santa for gifts?"

He glanced at their mom, who rolled her eyes. He'd

help her out. "I guess. But Jesus is the greater gift giver, so I ask Him."

The woman laid a hand on her chest and mouthed, "Thank you." He gave her a nod and they stepped up and placed their orders. By the time he grabbed his popcorn and two Cokes, the parade was in full swing.

"Where's Poppy?" he asked Delilah as he approached and handed her popcorn and a drink.

"She slipped off about ten, maybe fifteen minutes ago. She got a phone call then bolted toward the candle shop."

He handed Beth the other popcorn and drink. "I'll be back. If you see her, call me." Since the train incident, she had both their numbers now. He slipped through the crowd, calling Poppy's phone. Voice mail. Irritation replaced the tender feeling that had been inside him only seconds ago. How many times did he tell her not to go off half-cocked? The past couple of days she'd acquiesced to his warnings and let him take the lead. She was proving she could follow orders and be methodical and cautious.

Rhett should have known it wouldn't last, and now his heart jackhammered against his ribs. In this crazy crowd, with all the noise and hoopla, it wouldn't be difficult to make off with someone and no one notice. Everybody's attention was on Main Street. Why didn't she call him and tell him where she was going?

Because she was impulsive and hardheaded. That was the crux of why he'd pushed against being drawn to her, but it had backfired regardless of his efforts. Poppy had slipped right past his carefully constructed walls and gotten the jump on him.

He approached the candle store, but it was closed for

the parade. He checked the door to be sure. Locked. She hadn't gone inside, then. Snagging the toe of his shoe on the cobblestone, he grimaced but hurried behind the building. Nothing but parked vehicles and a Dumpster.

He called her phone again and the shrill timbre sounded nearby. Blood pooled in his brain, leaving him lightheaded. Following the rings, he found her phone behind the big Dumpster. He pocketed it and surveyed his surroundings.

She would never leave her phone on purpose.

With shaking hands, he called Sheriff Pritchard. Voice mail again. Would no one answer their phone today? Yet he knew the sheriff might be working crowd control and couldn't hear his phone.

He tried again. No answer. Frustration burned his gut.

He attempted Detective Teague, who answered on the second ring. "Agent Wallace. Please tell me you're with Agent Holliday."

Rhett's stomach sank. "No. Why?"

Teague relayed his phone call with her earlier and that she'd postponed the conversation to tail Solomon Simms.

"I'm afraid she's been taken."

"Have you called Rudy?"

"He's not answering—that's why I called you."

"He's technically not on duty today but I saw him here earlier. Try again. Look, I'm Santa for today, or I'd help you search. Call Detective Banner." He gave him Monty's cell phone number. "He's around here too with his sister somewhere."

He wanted to call in the National Guard. "If you see anything at all, call me." As he raced down sidewalks behind buildings, he prayed he would find her. He tried Monty's cell phone. Voice mail. Then he continued to call Sheriff Pritchard to no avail.

Why wouldn't he pick up his phone?

FOURTEEN

Poppy's body was being jostled as her captor and soon-to-be killer carried her concealed body.

"You know, Poppy," he said, "I'm not a bad man. I'm really not. I'm in a Santa suit! I'm a family man. I guess you know that was your partner on the phone. He's looking for you. I'm sure he'll be broken up about it when he can't find you. He's a nice guy and good agent. I feel bad for him."

Poppy couldn't ask Brad Teague all the questions she wanted to, like was Savannah in on it with him? Who killed Cora? How deep in was his wife?

"The truth is I had no idea about Cora or what happened that night. All of that went down before I moved to Gray Creek."

Poppy's body jostled and bumped against his back as he toted her in the Santa sack meant to hold gifts for children. Nope, just a dying woman in here.

"Rudy called me about a body in a well and I went out to the scene. When I got home and told Savannah what we'd found, she freaked out and confessed. I knew she'd done some spiteful things in school, but I had no idea she'd plotted to turn Dylan's affections away from your sister. But when she told me she'd dropped her ring down the well when they threw your sister down, I knew I could lose my family—it was Savannah who crushed the pill and put it in Cora's soft drink. I went out there to retrieve it but you were there. Already ruining everything."

He greeted people by name and ho-ho-ho-ed, laughing with citizens as if he weren't hauling a paralyzed woman over his shoulder. Several pillows covered her, rounding out the bag. No one would realize a body was inside. Poppy couldn't even cry—her tear ducts wouldn't work, but she felt the burning sensation of her dry eyes. Blinking was becoming more difficult.

"I was going to kill you, then go back for the ring, but that plan got messed up too," he growled. A door slammed shut. He must be inside the center now. "Man, this suit is hot and you're no lightweight."

It was becoming harder to breathe.

"When I got home that night, with the bad news that the ring was still in the well and you were here to re-open the case, I found Dylan in my front hall, dead. He'd heard the news and wanted to come forward. He wanted all of them to confess. She's a wife and a mother now. No longer that girl. She panicked and hit him. So I had to fix that situation too, but it was worth it because Savannah saved me all those years ago. I had no one after my mom died. I was so lost. Until Savannah found me."

Water ran from a faucet. They must be in a bathroom. The smell of his expensive cologne wafted into the bag. He must be freshening up. Carrying a woman who weighed a good 130 pounds wasn't a cakewalk. The beard she'd felt must have been his Santa beard, and the down of his coat the Santa costume.

"When we pulled up evidence, I saw the ring and pocketed it. I didn't know about a bracelet or I'd have taken that too."

What was Teague's endgame? To use Simms and frame him? Frame Ian? She was going to die without giving her family closure and peace. She'd never have the chance to admit out loud that she was in love with Rhett and probably had been for a long time without allowing herself to realize it. He'd blame himself for losing her, for her death, even though it was no more his fault than Keith's death had been.

She'd made the impulsive decision to follow Simms instead of waiting on Rhett or even calling him for fear he'd tell her to wait, and then Simms would have given her the slip. They'd timed it that way, she suddenly realized. Waited for the mild-mannered, cool-headed agent to leave and then appear before the hotheaded, impulsive agent. Teague knew she'd follow. Wouldn't wait.

"Okay, it's showtime. I hate the way this is going down. I'm not a killer by nature. But you have to go with me into Santa's Village. If I'm not there, your partner will put it together. He's smart. You aren't nearly as bright, but it's the obsession driving you. I knew you'd take the bait when you saw Simms."

Teague was a smart man himself. Inserted himself when needed and backed away at other times. Knew how to play them all.

She was lifted and hauled over his shoulder again. Voices grew louder, then kids cheered and hollered, "Santa!" while clapping. Teague let out his best Santa laugh, and she had to admit it was the best she'd ever heard. She was lowered to the floor, and he nudged her with his foot. What kind of monster was going to allow kids on his lap while his victim slowly died at his feet?

Breathing was increasingly difficult; only shallow pants came as her lungs began to slowly paralyze. Panic kicked in another round and she couldn't even shiver or shake, though she was more terrified than she'd ever been in her life.

"Well, hello there, Beth!"

"You know my name, Santa?"

Beth! Beth was having her picture made with a killer and would never know that Poppy was in the picture with her—only hidden. At least a piece of Poppy would always be with her. She'd quickly become attached to the sweet lady.

"What do you want for Christmas? What's your wish?" he asked with way more of a jolly attitude than a killer should possess.

"My wish this year isn't for me. Is that okay, Santa?"

"Oh yes. Giving is much better than receiving."

Poppy wanted to puke.

"My wish then is for my new friend Poppy."

Me? Poppy's heart sank. No point wasting her wish on a dead woman, but it deeply touched her that Beth would think of her.

"Oh?" Brad asked, and his boot nudged her again. If she had use of her muscles...

"Yes. I wish she wouldn't be sad anymore, and that she would feel God's hugs. 'Cause He loves her and He wants her to have Christmas joy again."

If Poppy could cry, she'd be a sobbing mess. Well, she could give Beth a last wish too, but not to Santa, who wasn't real. But to God. If she prayed. It had been so long since she really talked to God, trusted Him.

She'd been going through the motions for the benefit of loved ones, but not for herself.

And since Cora died, Poppy had no peace. No joy.

Along the way she'd stopped allowing herself to feel God's hugs, because she didn't believe He'd want to hug her anymore, and with every rebellious choice she made she assumed He loved her less and less to go along with the initial disappointment in her for her part in Cora's death.

But Beth was right.

God loved her.

He came because He loved. He died because He loved. And He was coming back because He loved.

But Poppy hadn't loved herself.

God, forgive me. I've wasted so much time believing my own lies. Other people's lies. I'm loved. No matter what I said. What I did. No matter how many times I was jealous of a sister who had a medical problem... I'm loved. By You.

Here in this bag, with her breath leaving her body, silently screaming for oxygen, she felt peace wash over her.

Felt the invisible hug of Jesus Christ warm her heart, which was well on its way to stilling.

The last words she'd hear were those of Beth Cordray. As if God wanted her to hear them now. To know them now. That she wasn't alone in this velvet bag.

God was with her. He knew precisely where she was. He knew exactly what she was going through. And whether she lived or died, He was with her and not abandoning her and He never had.

Cora... I'll see you soon, sis...

* * *

Rhett raced toward Santa's Village. He needed backup, and Santa would have to take a break and help him search. Poppy's life was at stake! He pushed through people and spotted Rudy Pritchard. "Hey!" he hollered and waved until he got his attention. Running over, he was ready to punch the guy for not answering his phone. "Never heard of picking up your phone, you jerk?"

Rudy scowled and glanced down.

Rhett noticed a little girl about seven or eight holding Rudy's hand. A little girl with Down syndrome. That explained his kindness and gentleness with Beth the night of the explosion.

"I'll ask you to watch your tone, Agent. I'm off duty and with my daughter."

Blinking, Rhett pulled his frantic self together. "Hello," he said to the little girl, then addressed the sheriff. "I'm sorry. It's Poppy. I found her phone. She's missing. He's got her. Solomon Simms. Teague said Solomon was dangerous and responsible for Cora's death."

Rudy frowned and looked down at his daughter.

"We need to pull Teague off Santa duty."

Rudy knelt in front of his daughter and cradled her face. "I have to go help find a lost lady. Can you stay here with Miss Shelley?"

She nodded and hugged him. Rhett recognized the woman standing with the sheriff from the popcorn stand. Her two kids were grabbing candy at the street's edge. "Hello again."

"Hello," he managed. Poppy was the only thing on his mind and time was running out. They left the crowd and sprinted toward Santa's Village.

"We'll find her," Rudy said.

They entered Santa's Village. On his lap Teague had a little boy in a cowboy hat who didn't seem thrilled to be there. He was squirming while Teague tried to calm him. Rhett caught his eye and waved. The boy slid from Teague's lap and tripped over Santa's sack, opening the mouth.

If Rhett wasn't in a state of panic, he'd have laughed at the ridiculous display as Teague scrambled to close the sack, but something caught Rhett's eye. He stepped forward, then began moving closer to Teague, who glanced up and paused, catching his eye again.

Green the color of Poppy's sweater poked through a pillow's edge in the sack. Rhett turned and hollered, "It's Brad!"

Brad hurdled over the velvet bag and shot out back, Rudy hot on his tail.

Kids cried and parents murmured. Sliding to the floor, Rhett peered into the bag, using discretion to keep the children from being traumatized further. Santa had fled the building.

Poppy lay in a heap, staring at him with wide, lifeless eyes.

No. No. No.

"Clear out! We...we have an emergency with the reindeer. Everybody out!" Adults caught on and rushed their children from the building.

Paramedics arrived, running toward him. Rudy must have radioed them.

With trembling hands, Rhett carefully withdrew Poppy from the red velvet Santa sack and cradled her lifeless body, feeling for a pulse but he couldn't find one.

"No, you can't be gone. You can't leave me without a fight or a single snide remark, Poppy Holliday." He laid his forehead against hers, his heart breaking in small pieces. "I love you. I don't care that we're colleagues. Because it wouldn't have ended badly. It wouldn't have ended at all."

He'd been so stupid to hold back out of fear. Now a greater fear had come true. He laid her out to begin compressions. To attempt to revive her. Anything. He'd do anything.

He'd give up structure and order. Take a risk, take a chance. But it was too late.

God, please revive her. Give us another chance.

"Sir, let us through," a paramedic said. Pushing Rhett aside, they knelt and went to work on her.

Moisture filled his eyes as he stared into Poppy's unblinking eyes. "Please, please bring her back. I love that woman. I can't lose her. Please help her."

The woman working on her frowned, then grew wide-eyed. "She's not dead. I've seen this before," she said to the other paramedic. "Rape case two years ago in Oxford. She's not dead—she's paralyzed. I need a line! We're gonna lose her."

Everything happened so fast and in slow motion.

Poppy was alive. Alive!

For now.

Rhett walked into Poppy's hospital room. The doctors had been able to save her and bring her out of paralysis. Rhett had called their unit chief, Colt, and the team. Then he'd called her brother Tack. Poppy's cell phone password had been easy to figure out—Cora's birthday.

Rudy had caught Brad and had him, Solomon Simms, Savannah Steadman-Teague, Natalie Carpenter-Weaverman and Ian Kirkwood in custody. Brad had run, thinking he could get to Savannah and his family and get out of the country.

Savannah had no choice but to admit she'd accidentally killed Cora because Ian and Natalie were now talking and hoping for plea deals.

"You can see her now," a nurse said.

It was after midnight. Officially Christmas. Rhett tiptoed inside and stood at the foot of Poppy's bed. She was pale and asleep. But alive.

Her eyes fluttered open as if she sensed his presence. She took his fingers in her weak hand and squeezed. "Did you get him?"

"We got him," he whispered. "Natalie and Ian said it went down like Solomon Simms told us. Maya was seeing him and she did go to him that night and confess. The death was an accident and they panicked. It was Savannah who came up with the idea to throw Cora down the well, then they made a pact to never speak of it again, but Dylan balked. They finally talked him into it, but it took a toll on him."

"Savannah killed Dylan, and Brad made it look like an accident or suicide—doubtful he cared which. They can spray luminol for blood evidence in Savannah's foyer. He told me what he did. He was going to put me in that well, Rhett."

He kissed her hand. "No one is going to hurt you now, Poppy."

She closed her eyes and nodded. "They're being charged?"

"Savannah for manslaughter and murder in the second degree—for Dylan. She knew what Brad was up to. She admitted to calling him in the hall at the mansion and leaving on purpose to give herself an alibi when he showed up and shoved you down the broken elevator shaft. She was in on the frame-up."

Poppy squeezed her eyes shut. "And the others?"

"Ian and Natalie are being charged as accessories to murder. Brad is being charged for attempted murder and murdering Maya, along with tampering with evidence and anything else the DA can get him on. Zack admitted to lying about Dylan's alibi. He wasn't sure what Dylan had been a part of, but he believed Dylan when he insisted he had nothing to do with Cora's death. And he hadn't." He'd been tortured internally all these years with a horrible secret. "Zack has suspected Natalie and Dylan of an affair over the years, even though they'd denied it the few times he'd asked. It wasn't until after you showed him the photo of the bracelet he knew what had bonded them so tightly—they were keeping each other held together by a thin thread over Cora's murder. But he kept silent to protect Natalie."

"What about Solomon Simms? Is he terminally ill or not?"

"No. He did have cancer and he is in remission. He and Maya still see each other sometimes—even if she was seeing Monty. I guess her confession to him, and the fact he'd taken advantage of her so young, created a twisted bond between them."

"He's still actively growing and distributing marijuana. I heard him say it."

"I think Brad and Savannah wanted to pin everything on Simms and get Ian and Natalie to go along with it, which I think they would have. But according to

Simms, Brad was pinning the murders on Ian. I believe Brad lied to Simms and had plans to make it look like he killed Cora and had an interest in her. She refused the advances and threatened to tell. But Maya wouldn't go along with that because she still loved Simms. So Teague killed her and told Simms that Ian did it. It worked out nicely for Teague that Ian had shown up for animal meds, really sold it to Simms. He thought he was helping Teague set up Ian Kirkwood, but actually they were setting up Simms. It might have worked too."

"And to think, if it hadn't been for a bratty kid accidentally knocking open the Santa sack…" Poppy's eyes closed and her head rolled to the side, but a smile graced her gorgeous face.

Rhett softly kissed her forehead. They had more to talk about.

Much more.

Once she rested.

"Merry Christmas, Poppy," he whispered.

FIFTEEN

Poppy had been released from the hospital a little after noon. This would be another Christmas she'd never forget. The year Santa abducted and tried to murder her. She'd walked into the B&B and been stunned by the full house of people. Her whole family had flown in— Mom, Dad, all of her brothers. Tack had shaken his head and congratulated her for not being careful and watching her back like he'd told her to, but wrapped her up in a big bear hug.

And Rhett's family was there too. He looked like his dad. He was going to age nicely.

Even her cold case unit had flown in from the mountains and the islands. Colt and Georgia. Mae and Cash. She couldn't believe they'd cut their honeymoon short for her, but she was thankful and moved. Poppy had never been hugged and loved on so much in her life, and there was no doubt that God was in every single arm that embraced her.

When she had a moment alone with her parents, she confessed the argument, her jealousies and her shame. She admitted how unloved she'd felt, and for the first time in her life, she saw her military father cry. She hadn't even witnessed it when Cora died—though he surely had shed tears in private.

Her parents had always loved her, but confessed too that although sometimes Poppy and the boys took the backburner, they never loved Cora more, nor did they ever blame Poppy. But in Poppy's own guilt and shame, she'd misinterpreted their grief. Saw what she wanted based on the lies she believed about herself and assumed her parents thought the same.

Delilah had been thrilled to have her home brimming with company, and she had plenty of room for everyone. Mom and Rhett's mother helped Delilah prepare the meal and they'd all eaten together. Family. Togetherness. Everything Christmas should be, but hadn't been in many years.

But even if Poppy had been alone, she wasn't truly alone.

She and Rhett hadn't had a chance to talk in private but it appeared he'd had some kind of reunion with his own family, and his mother had hugged her in a way that made her wonder exactly what Rhett had told her about Poppy.

Needing a minute to breathe—now that she actually could—she'd come upstairs to her room. She retrieved Rhett's gift from under the bed. Beth had loved her presents and had made Poppy a pinecone wreath as a gift, but Beth was Poppy's best Christmas gift. She'd been the bridge back to her faith. It was Poppy who had to cross it, but it might still be burned to ash if not for the precious woman with more wisdom and pure joy than anyone she'd ever met.

A light knock sounded. "Come in."

Rhett opened the door and slipped inside, closing it behind him. "How you feeling?" he asked.

"Better. Overwhelmed. Alive." In so many ways.

"You look amazing. It couldn't have been an easy haul for Teague with you in that sack. I know how heavy you are." He winked and she laughed.

"Rhett the stiff shirt, tossing out jokes."

"I know you know it's stuffed shirt."

"I do." She stood and closed the distance between them. "I know a lot of things." Like the fact he'd told her he loved her when he pulled her from that bag. Would he tell her again? Strange how it took her being forced to be still to listen, and what she heard in those moments was the best thing she'd ever heard.

"I know you do." He sighed. "I got you something." He handed her a wrapped present from behind his back. "Open it."

She grinned and ripped off the paper and held up a T-shirt that read I Do What I Want. I Say What I Want. Get over It. Laughing, she held it up to her.

"It felt appropriate at the time I saw it."

"I made some bad decisions doing what I want. I'm sorry for not calling you first. For not taking the measured steps you tried to drill into me." She loved the shirt but… "I'm not sure I'm this person anymore." She grabbed his gift from the bed. "I got you something too."

He cocked his head with a skeptical expression, but opened the wooden sign that said he was silently correcting her grammar. She'd marked out "Grammar" and written *"Idioms"* in a permanent marker. Rhett laughed and shook his head. "So true." He studied the plaque then looked at Poppy. "After Keith died, I was afraid to take chances—any chance that might have a negative consequence. Got into a routine. I'm not sure I'm this man anymore." He held up the plaque.

"What do we do about that?" Poppy asked.

He laid the present on the edge of the bed and framed her face. "I love you, Poppy. I think I have for a really long time. And I know you know this because the doctor told me you were paralyzed but in full control of your faculties." He grinned.

"I do. And it gave me hope and a reason to fight to live. Because I love you too, and I think I have for a really long time."

He brushed his thumb across her cheek. "Good. 'Cause I plan to be here for the long haul." He drew her into his arms. She loved this place best. Against him, warm and secure.

"If you make a joke about how much I weigh—"

He cut her off with a kiss that proved every word he said and sealed it with a promise for forever. Partnership in every way.

"Merry Christmas," he whispered against her lips. "I'll get you a much more elaborate gift next Christmas."

Poppy pecked his lips. "If you're referring to a ring, Valentine's is coming up sooner."

He laughed. "I think you could still wear the shirt and get away with it." He kissed her again and trailed his lips along her jaw to her ear. "But I agree about Valentine's," he breathed.

Poppy hadn't been this happy, this full of joy and faith in a long time.

She glanced up and knew Cora would be happy for her.

* * * * *

*If you enjoyed this story, pick up the
previous books in Jessica R. Patch's
Cold Case Investigators miniseries:*

Cold Case Takedown
Cold Case Double Cross

*Available now from
Love Inspired Suspense!*

And look for Jessica R. Patch's next release,

Her Darkest Secret

*Available from
Love Inspired Trade in April 2022!*

Dear Reader,

This story took on a life of its own, and I knew it was going to be special. Maybe you can relate to Poppy and Rhett. Both felt responsible for the loss of their loved ones and both had a hard time forgiving themselves. I don't know what you might be going through or feeling guilty about, but God loves you and if you ask for forgiveness, He gives it freely.

I hope you enjoyed this story. I'd love for you to come find and follow me on BookBub, and feel free to email me or sign up for my newsletter at my website: www.jessicarpatch.com

Jessica R. Patch

COMING NEXT MONTH FROM
Love Inspired Suspense

BLIZZARD SHOWDOWN
Alaska K-9 Unit • by Shirlee McCoy
After months of searching for Violet James, Gabriel Runyon and his K-9 partner finally track her down—just in time to rescue her from her ex-fiancé. Now it's up to them to safeguard the single mother and her newborn daughter. But can they outrun a blizzard *and* an enemy who wants Violet dead?

CHRISTMAS K-9 PROTECTORS
Alaska K-9 Unit • by Lenora Worth and Maggie K. Black
Members of the K-9 team face danger and find love in these holiday novellas, in which a rookie K-9 trooper and his furry partner must save a forensic scientist from a ruthless jewelry thief, and a tech whiz, a criminal psychologist and a K-9 go on the run to keep a teen out of the hands of a kidnapping gang.

AMISH CHRISTMAS ESCAPE
Amish Country Justice • by Dana R. Lynn
In the sights of a murderer, Christy O'Malley knows there is just one person she can rely on to shield her—her estranged husband, who doesn't know he is a father. But when she shows up on Sam Burkholder's doorstep in Amish country, can he help her and their little girl live through Christmas?

CHRISTMAS VENDETTA
Emergency Responders • by Valerie Hansen
Teacher Sandy Lynn Forrester's peaceful Christmas vacation is interrupted when somebody tries to kill her—but the cops don't think the threat is real. The only person who believes her is a man she doesn't trust: framed and discredited cop Clay Danforth. But with her life on the line, he's her best chance at survival...

CAPTURED AT CHRISTMAS
by Jodie Bailey
Undercover with an infantry unit to investigate the theft of hard drives, military investigator Captain Rachel Blake doesn't expect the holiday assignment to turn into a protection mission. But when Captain Marshall Slater and his little girl are targeted, she'll risk everything to help keep them safe.

WYOMING CHRISTMAS PERIL
by Kathie Ridings
Fleeing from a murderous bank robber at Christmastime, Bailey O'Keefe has only FBI agent Sean Hanson to protect her. But when their safe house is breached, can Bailey and Sean outmaneuver their enemy while battling the elements and the hazards of the snow-packed trails on Cougar Mountain?

LOOK FOR THESE AND OTHER LOVE INSPIRED BOOKS WHEREVER BOOKS ARE SOLD, INCLUDING MOST BOOKSTORES, SUPERMARKETS, DISCOUNT STORES AND DRUGSTORES.

LISCNM1121

Sounds of a scuffle woke Clay Danforth. He stared up at the ceiling and saw the light fixture vibrate. Whatever was happening on the floor above him was violent, which did not bode well for the residents of that apartment.

He listened carefully, seeking confirmation of his initial conclusion. It came in the form of a woman's scream. It didn't matter that he hadn't yet met his neighbors. Somebody up there needed him, and although his authority had ended when he'd left the police force, his concern for fellow citizens had not. He pulled on jeans and boots, palmed his phone long enough to call 911, then slipped a gun into the waistband at the small of his back and headed for the stairway.

Taking the steps two at a time, he rounded the corner and saw a partially open door. Raised voices identified that apartment as the source of the conflict. A woman's screeching demand to be left alone spurred him into a run.

Slamming his shoulder against the outer wall next to the doorjamb, he drew the gun. "Police! Come out with your hands up."

In moments a black-clad figure raced past him and pounded down the stairs. Without knowing any details, Clay didn't dare shoot; nor was it prudent to give chase.

Anticipating a second criminal or more, Clay whipped around the corner and took a shooter's stance in the doorway. Something whizzed past his ear and clipped the edge of his shoulder. "Stop! I'm a police officer." Which was sort of still true.

He diverted his aim. His free hand shot out to grab the metal shaft of the club. When he focused on the person holding the leather grip, the effect was mind-blowing. Looking into those familiar hazel eyes, he croaked, "Sandy?"

The impossibility that he would have chosen an apartment directly beneath Sandy Lynn Forrester, the one woman who had shattered his heart into a thousand pieces, was not only astounding, but it made him furious with the friend who had talked him into the lease. He would never have listened to Abe and signed the contract if he'd dreamed she lived in the same building. Never in a million years.

Don't miss
Christmas Vendetta *by Valerie Hansen,*
available December 2021 wherever
Love Inspired Suspense books and ebooks are sold.

LoveInspired.com

**IF YOU ENJOYED THIS BOOK
WE THINK YOU WILL ALSO LOVE**

LOVE INSPIRED COLD CASE
INSPIRATIONAL ROMANCE

Courage. Danger. Faith.

Be inspired by compelling stories where past crimes are
investigated and criminals are brought to justice.

AVAILABLE NOVEMBER 30, 2021